I0580649

Fragments of Goodbye

Cora Whitmore

Copyright © 2024 by Cora Whitmore

All rights reserved.

No portion of this book may be reproduced in any form without written permission from the publisher or author, except as permitted by U.S. copyright law.

Contents

1. Prologue   1

2. Chapter 1   4

3. Chapter 2   11

4. Chapter 3   16

5. Chapter 4   22

6. Chapter 5   30

7. Chapter 6   35

8. Chapter 7   40

9. Chapter 8   44

10. Chapter 9   49

11. Chapter 10   54

12. Chapter 11   59

13. Chapter 12   66

14. Chapter 13   71

15. Chapter 14   76

16. Chapter 15   81

17. Chapter 16   87

18. Chapter 17   93

19. Chapter 18   100

20. Chapter 19   106

21. Chapter 20   115

22. Chapter 21   119

23. Chapter 22   124

24. Chapter 23   129

25. Chapter 24   134

26. Chapter 25   139

27. Chapter 26   144

28. Chapter 27   151

29. Chapter 28   157

30. Chapter 29   166

31. Chapter 30   174

32. Chapter 31   179

33. Chapter 32   186

34. Chapter 33   192

35. Chapter 34   199

36. Chapter 35   204

37. Chapter 36   211

38. Chapter 37   216

39. Chapter 38   222

40. Epilogue   226

Prologue

They told me I was going to survive without her. One day, she will be nothing but a memory, or so they say. Everyone said it would be okay. None of them could tell me how to move on, but they say it is possible, even though they don't know when the process starts or how it will begin. I was alone with my thoughts, again. All anybody could say was it was for the better.

I felt sixteen again, snorting whatever the man I met on the streets had in his pocket for a low price. Las Vegas got me high, but she made me feel low. Since arriving, every morning, I wake up to another warm body next to mine. The curls spread against the pillow weren't enough to soothe the discomfort. They weren't soft enough. They weren't curly enough. They weren't her.

No matter how many hours I spent between someone else's legs, I couldn't bury the emotions coursing through my veins. Their body didn't mold against mine, and when my thumb grazed their hips, I didn't feel the scar from that stupid fucking shopping cart incident she was in.

I tried to fill the pieces, but the girls from Vegas weren't what was missing. The curly-haired girl with caramel eyes kept me whole. And as I try to make myself feel complete again, I am staring down a white line on the table with shaky hands before my fight because I know she won't be there. I know she wouldn't be in the seat reserved just for her, wearing the t-shirt with my name on the back. She wouldn't be there to remind me what I was fighting for.

And when I stepped into the arena, my head could barely stay straight. John screamed at me from one side of the room, causing the pounding in my head to intensify. I pressed the bottle of alcohol to my lips, finishing off the cheap vodka from the corner store, before tossing it into the trashcan next to me. I wasn't sure if my chest was on fire from the liquid that tasted like rubbing alcohol or the inability to remember how many drugs I snorted before climbing into the suburban that brought me here.

My body tensed as fingers gripped my cheeks. "Look at me, kid."

I tried to focus on John as he kept my head still. "What did you take, Kinnick?"

"Nothing that is working," I mumbled. "I need something stronger."

"You have been sober for three years," his voice cracked.

My shoulders shrugged as my back fell against the cement wall. "I can't find a reason anymore."

John turned around, looking back toward the men behind him. "Call it off. Tell them we are forfeiting the match."

"What?" I snapped. "No -"

"Get Jimmy's number," he said without listening to me. "Tell him I will pay whatever I have to -"

"Jimmy?" My body struggled to stand. "I am not going back there!"

"You need help!" A tear strayed from John's eye as he stared at me. "Do you know how many times I almost lost you? I won't go through that again! I am not your fucking parents, Kinnick. I will not sit back and watch you ruin everything you have worked for! I won't let you kill yourself!"

Before I could say another word, everything came up. John called out to someone for a rag as he pulled the trashcan over to me. As the bitter burn of Vodka continued to pour into the container in front of me, John talked to someone on the phone.

"John," I laid over the trashcan. "I'll do whatever you want, but don't send me back there."

"Kinnick, you can barely keep your head up."

"I'll come to stay with you," I winced at the taste in my mouth. "Whatever you want. Just don't take me to Jimmy. I can't go there again."

"He helped you -"

"I can't be alone with everything that is on my mind, John," tears welled in my eyes as I slipped out of consciousness. "Please."

"We need to get him to a hospital," someone's voice called through the room.

"Somebody help!" A voice boomed through the hallway. "We need help!"

Just as I felt the weakness flush through my body and I wasn't strong enough to keep myself up anymore, I collapsed to the ground. As my eyes fluttered, I felt John turning me to sit straight. Before everything went black, I heard him begging like he did every time I fucked up -

"Please, don't take him from me."

Chapter 1

The therapist told me to find something to keep me grounded whenever my feet started to rise. Even if the clouds were beautiful, we didn't live up there. Our life exists down here, and I need to stop looking for a getaway whenever the pain becomes too much. She told me I had to get better for myself. Sobriety won't work if I rely on someone else because I am the only thing in my life that remains constant. Well, I guess it has kind of worked because I have been sober since the night John begged whoever it was he cried too to keep me alive.

And I didn't start therapy because John begged me to, even if he did. The court system ordered it. After my lawyer assured the judge my childhood trauma was the reason for fracturing a man's eye socket. Not only did I have to pay for the surgery he endured after breaking it in three different places, but I was reminded of how I shattered his jaw. They installed metal plates to reinforce his bone structure, and I don't even remember what started the fight because I drank so much I could barely recall my name.

It isn't like I hear about it every time I step onto the streets, but it wasn't as if people didn't hate me before everything happened either. That didn't stop my anxiety from eating at me whenever I wondered about Bo and if she heard about what happened. Ninety percent of the time, I couldn't stand myself. I couldn't expect any less from her.

Somehow I drifted away from the gym, and it has been over a year since I slipped into a pair of gloves. When my eyes dropped to my knuckles, I couldn't lie and say it has been that long since I fought somebody because the bar incident only happened a few weeks ago. Now I am just a washed-up boxer who had it all but let it slip right through his fingertips.

So, as I was saying, the therapist told me to find something to keep me grounded. I should have been healing from the pain that Bo caused, but healing starts with accepting, and I finally accepted that she didn't do anything wrong. I killed her mom, and I don't know how to live with myself. Instead of forgetting her because I knew it would never happen, I got a tattoo.

Whenever the pain became too much, I would look down at the typewriter lettering on the side of my wrist that said the word, Yellow. Her favorite color and the one thing my life revolves around now. I could practically live in it -

"How was therapy?" Trevor slid a white mug toward me.

My shoulders lifted slightly as I stared at the coffee below me. I didn't feel different, just more like shit than before. The guilt has been weighing heavy on my shoulders, and when it started to hit me, I didn't have a defense mechanism. So, I stared over the word etched into my skin as I hoped for relief.

"Did you get the paperwork I asked for?" I lifted my eyes as I brought the mug to my lips.

"They are on your desk," he wiped down the counter with his white rag. "They have been increasing. We have made more money this week than we did last year in a whole month."

The black coffee fell down my throat as I nodded. "Thank you."

As I slid off of the barstool, I picked up the mug to take with me. The anxiety rising in my stomach made me feel nauseous, but before I could round the corner to get away, Trevor called out to me. My eyebrows perked up as I stared at him with confusion.

"Are you okay?"

I swallowed harshly. "Yeah."

"You can stay out here," he nodded toward the barstool as he looked at me. "Everything is okay between us."

My head moved back and forth. "No, it's not."

"I forgave you a while ago -"

"I can't forgive myself."

"Kinnick -"

"Tell me when everyone is here, yeah?"

The office door slammed shut behind me as I finished off the rest of my coffee. My fingers curled around the handle as I did what I could to stop myself from chucking the porcelain against the wall. I slid it onto my desk before walking toward the couch in front of my desk to sit down. As my fingers raked through my hair, I tried stopping the memories of what happened, but I couldn't.

I sucked in deep breaths as flashbacks of the party started playing in my head. It didn't matter to me that Trevor was outside, serving drinks at the bar. After taking shots together, I pulled his girlfriend to my office. Her fingers ripped at my button-down as I lifted her on my desk.

The amount of alcohol I drank wasn't an excuse. Down the hall from where he worked, I fucked his girlfriend, and I couldn't blame anything but myself. It didn't matter how willing she was; I shouldn't have let it happen. After it happened, we left the room, and Trevor didn't need to ask to know. He could tell.

The worst part? He didn't say a word. I watched him walk out of the bar, and as everyone yelled at me for being a piece of shit, I continued drinking. When Monday rolled around, he came back to work. And what hurts the most is watching him walk through my office door the same day with dark circles under his eyes, asking if I was okay. I couldn't understand it, but he told me that recovery makes you different.

When my door creaked open, my head snapped up to see Trevor coming through with the pot of coffee in his hands. "I figured you wanted this."

I swallowed harshly as my eyes burned. "Thanks."

"It hurt me when it happened," he cleared his throat. "But I know you, and my best friend wouldn't have done that to me."

"But your best friend did do that to you -"

"No," Trevor's head moved back and forth. "I've been there, Kin-nick. Sobriety isn't easy. You will never be more lost in your life than you are in those first few months."

"I won't use it as an excuse -"

"You don't have to," his voice sounded heavy. "But if that is what you needed to feel okay, even if it was for a few minutes, I am okay with that."

"Why can't you be less understanding?" I snapped. "Why don't you hit me or scream at me? Fucking do something other than stand before and accept everything I did to you!"

"Because that isn't me," his voice remained the same. "And you know that."

"I just want what I deserve."

"You can't find peace if you continue letting the past affect your future."

"What are you, my fucking therapist?"

"Well, obviously," he rolled his eyes. "It is clear that the one you have isn't doing good enough."

The corner of my lips tugged upward as he sassed me back. A chuckle emitted from his lips as I stared up at him. Another rumble came from my chest as he started laughing harder. Just as I was about to tell him how sorry I was for what happened, his head began to move back and forth.

"I don't want to hear it."

Before he could process another moment, I stood from the couch. My arms wrapped around him as I brought him into my chest. I felt his hesitation before his hold secured me. When I pulled away, his eyes were wide with confusion.

"I am sorry anyway," I patted his shoulder. "I just want you to know that."

As I left him alone to stand in my office, I came around the corner to see my servers greeting guests. When John walked through the doors with Riley at his side, a smile grew on my face. My former trainer walked toward me with a grin, opening his arms for me as I walked toward him.

"How are you doing, kid?" He mumbled into my shoulder.

"I am doing good," I nodded. "How are you two?"

"We are doing great," the stubble on his face moved with his smile. "Is everyone here yet?"

My head moved back and forth before seeing Miles walking in with Chrissy by his side. "Nevermind, here they are."

"Good," he placed a hand on Riley's back. "Let's go sit down."

As we slid around the table, my mood began to deteriorate at the sight of the woman in front of me. I watched as she did whatever she could to avoid my gaze. After what happened with Bo, she hasn't attempted to talk to me, and I would rather keep it that way. I couldn't stand her. Every little thing she did pissed me off.

"When did this happen?" I pointed between Chrissy and Miles.

Miles curled his fingers around Chrissy's hand. "A few months ago."

"You all just moved in together," John furrowed his eyebrows. "How has that been?"

The girl I couldn't stand frowned at John's question and started yet another story I didn't want to fucking listen to. "Weird. Bo is barely home."

When she said her name, I drowned myself with another glass of coffee. It just didn't work like whiskey did. As I poured my mug full again, John looked at me with concern. Everyone stopped talking as if they had to tip-toe around me. They didn't understand. I wanted to hear how she was doing; it just fucking hurt to know she was doing better without me. Even though it was exactly what I wanted to hear.

"I am sorry," Chrissy said without emotion.

I shake my head before letting my toxicity speak for me. "Don't fucking start - I am not fragile. You can say her name without me falling apart."

John ignored my attitude as he carried on with his conversation. "How is she doing after what happened?"

"What happened?" I snapped.

Chrissy became unbelievably quiet, and Miles's eyes wouldn't lift from his food. My hand reached for the gun strapped to my belt buckle. The leather burned against my fingers as I unfastened the metal. John rolled his eyes before leaning back into his seat and bringing the cup of orange juice to his lips to slowly sip on as he casually waited for my next move.

"Clearly, therapy isn't working," John mumbled.

I spoke with strain as I shoved the clip in. "Somebody needs to start talking."

Chapter 2

John tried to mediate the situation. He wasn't phased by the loaded gun in my hand until I slammed it on the table, and Riley jumped. He asked me to put the safety back on, but my eyes met his as I flicked it off. When his eyes rolled, and he sucked in a deep breath, I knew I was annoying him as much as I did every other time we were around one another. My head rolled to look back at Chrissy and Miles. Just as my chest started to heave with annoyance, I watched her lips part.

"You heard about her first case, right? Well, after winning, she went out to celebrate with a few people from her firm," Chrissy sighed. "I am not sure when they ended up going back to their office -"

"Someone attacked her in her office," Miles interrupted. "Nobody knows the whole story, but whoever it was hit her hard enough to crack her cheek open. She didn't tell anybody. I found out when I woke up to bloody footprints all over the floor."

"All we know is they demanded to see files from a previous case she looked into when she started, and they threatened to come back after her -"

"Where is she now?" I stared down at the table as my nails dug into my palms.

"Home," Miles said as if I should already know.

My hands collided with the table as everything I held back came out. "Are you fucking kidding me? You took her home!"

"What did you want me to do?" He snapped.

"Call me!"

"And say what? She wants nothing to do with me ninety percent of the time!"

"I don't give a fuck what she wants," I seethed. "You don't know who did it, which means you don't know what to look out for. When it comes to her safety and that fucker coming back, I could care less what she wants! And you are a fucking idiot for taking her back home!"

"Luke is there," Chrissy spoke up as if it would solve everything.

A smile crossed my face as I let out a deep breath. "You are joking right? Your brother, Luke?"

"Yeah -"

"What is he going to do? That kid isn't about shit and never has been," I spoke down to her. "Bo has a better chance at protecting herself."

"Luke wouldn't let anything happen to her -"

"I guess Warren didn't get the memo then, did he?"

Her mouth snapped shut before she regained herself. "He might not be able to protect her from everything, but look at who she ended up with in the end."

"Chrissy," Miles growled.

"No, speak up," I challenged.

Her blue eyes flashed with concern as my elbows connected with the table, and I leaned forward to look closer at her. Her lip twitched as if she would start crying, and I wanted to see her break. My palms smacked the table, letting an echo clap through the bar.

"Say it!"

"You were never jealous of Luke and you never thought you had anything to prove," a smirk grew on her lips as tears welled in her eyes. "But that is who Bo picked in the end. She chose your complete opposite. Someone who is worth -"

I snatched the gun off of the table and listened to the chairs around me screech as I cocked the hammer. Miles threw his arm in front of Christina as he sat on the edge of his seat, waiting for my next move. Before letting my fingertip glide over the trigger, I stood up from my spot. My fingers itched to pull the metal back and put an end to her excessive talking.

As she stared down the barrel of my gun, tears started to rapidly fall down her cheeks. I knew that if I pulled the trigger, that would be it. I would be everything Bo thought I was. My intentions weren't to kill her mom, but if I planted a bullet in her best friend's forehead, that would be a different story.

My glass shattered on the floor as the table rocked back and forth from the force of my shove. As I finished off the cup in my hand, I stalked off toward my office. As I heard footsteps behind me, I felt the shiver of fear on my back. I couldn't stop myself, not with a gun in my hand.

"Kinnick," Chrissy called after me.

I flipped around, pointing at her. "Quit while you are ahead, Christina."

"I am sorry -"

Before she could finish what she was saying, I rushed toward her. The whimpers leaving her lips said to let up, but my body shoved hers against the wall as I let my fist crack the wall beside her face. Her cheek was smashed against the surface behind her as she tried to get away from me, but my barricade wouldn't allow it to happen.

A sob broke through her lips as I stared down at her. "I told you to fucking stop and you don't listen. Let this be my last and final warning. I don't care if Bo is your best friend, you so much as talk to me in that tone you just did, and I'll shatter your jaw."

"You wouldn't hit me -"

"You don't know me," I seethed.

"Kinnick!" John barked from behind me as Miles grabbed Chrissy. "What is your problem? You need to -"

"She has been with him the whole time and you never said a fucking word," I turned to him with a burn growing in my throat. "She was attacked and nobody told me."

"Bo asked us not to-"

"Fuck you, John," I blew out a large breath. "Because you are the first person to preach about trust, and you want to keep shit away from me?"

"Kid," tears welled in his eyes.

"All of you can get the fuck out," I shake my head.

As their footsteps grew further away from me, I wiped my eyes free of any sign that I might be upset. The door to my office slammed shut as I stared at the couch before me—home sweet home. But it wasn't home at all. Home is a curly-haired girl with dimples in her smile. Home is Bo. Well, it was. And I lay awake again, asking myself the same question I do every night before I close my eyes, why the fuck am I still sober?

Chapter 3

O ne of my many failures in life was convincing Bo that it was okay to talk about the trauma in our lives because it would make the weight less heavy on our chest. She told me how talking to a therapist ruined that for her when they tried to admit her to a hospital. I wanted to change that for her and gain whatever trust she lost, but as I stared up at the judge, I understood how she felt.

My therapist sat before everyone, telling the judge that therapy wasn't working for me. She needed more time for everything to work. I realized telling her about what happened at the bar last week wasn't the best idea I had ever come up with because now it has come back to bite me in the ass.

As she stepped down from the stand, the judge turned to me with disgust in his eyes. I looked down at the ground because I had lived this scene so often that I knew what would happen before he said it.

My lawyer tried to protest that if therapy didn't work, I would find myself in a cell. Again. I stared down at my hands, realizing that I was turning out to be the man everyone said I would be. Instead of changing that, I continued letting it happen because I didn't know life outside of fucking everything up.

After the gavel came down, I stood up without taking a second look at my lawyer. He couldn't do anything for me. I wasn't sure what the fuck I was paying him for because he got me out the first time, and now I don't have much of a choice.

I looked at the empty seats behind me, noticing nobody cared to show up. It wasn't like I reached out to anybody because I couldn't expect them to show up after what happened. But if I was arrested, who would I have to say goodbye to? A series of chuckles made my head snap up to see who found my trouble hilarious.

Seth stood in his uniform, adjusting his button-down shirt. "Not much has changed, has it?"

I scoffed, shaking my head as the corners of my lips tugged upward. "Nope. You can still get dropped too."

"What is that? A threat?" He grinned. "I am not sure what you think you are capable of, but I have been hit by you before, it is nothing."

A snort emitted from my lips. "But you'll never step to me, and we both know that."

"You must think you are some tough guy, huh?" He looked up at me. "A guy is walking around with metal plates in his face and you walk away with court ordered therapy."

"Yeah," I swallowed harshly. "Something like that."

"I told you, you would never amount to anything," he said. "You have no meaning around here anymore."

"I didn't need you to tell me that," I shake my head. "It has been that way for years."

Before he could say another word, I walked away. I didn't need Seth to tell me how badly I fucked up. It has been happening for so long that I wake up in the morning wondering what I will do wrong the second I slip out of bed.

When I made it to my truck, I thought of ways to cancel lunch with John, but I knew if I wanted to apologize for what happened last week, I couldn't. So, as I pulled in front of the building to see him sitting inside with Riley, I worried about what would happen. How could I fuck this up more than I already did?

As I stepped through the entrance, he stood from his seat with a smile on his face. It made me wonder how everyone could be so understanding? John's arms wrapped around me as I stepped in front of him.

"How are you doing, kid?"

I nodded, sucking in a deep breath. "Good. I just got done at court."

"Why didn't you say anything? We would have been there."

"You don't need to spend any more time in a courthouse than what you already have."

"If you need support, I'll spend as long as I need to in a court-room."

I shake my head, chuckling. "It is okay, John."

"I ordered you a water," he pointed to the glass. "I wasn't sure what else you wanted."

"That is okay," I slid into the booth. "How are you doing, Riley?"

"Good," he gave me a soft smile.

"I am sorry for what happened," I cleared my throat. "It was out of hand."

"It is fine," Riley spoke before John. "We understand, Kinnick."

"I am trying to get help," I shake my head. "I really am, but I don't know if it is working."

"You want to get help," John smiled at me. "That is how you know it is working."

A smile pulled across my lips. "Yeah, I guess."

"We love you," they both looked at me. "Recovery sucks, kid, but you are doing great."

"Really? I keep feeling like I am fucking everything up," I sucked in a deep breath.

"Well, healing is messy," Riley spoke softly. "Nobody should have expectations of what it looks like because it is different for everybody."

I furrowed my eyebrows. "I love you guys."

A look of happiness stole John's features. "We love you more, and we have something we want to tell you."

"What?"

Riley lifted his hand, showing off his ring. "We got engaged!"

The corner of my lips tugged upward. "What?"

"We got engaged," John squealed. "We wanted you to be the first to know!"

Without saying another word, I stood up from my seat and threw my arms around his neck. John tightened his hold on me, rocking back and forth as he laughed with excitement. I couldn't stop the feelings from coursing through my body as my best friend expressed his emotions. When he pulled away, I knew something else was coming, and it made me nervous.

"We want you to come to our engagement party," he begged.

I furrowed my eyebrows. "Of course, I will be there."

"I don't want to ruin a good moment," he cleared his throat. "But I am inviting, Bo."

"It is your party," I shake my head. "You can invite whoever you want. I'll be fine."

"I wanted to tell you first," he frowned. "I just thought you needed to know."

"Does she know I am coming?"

He nodded. "I told her I was inviting you."

"Is she okay with it?"

"She didn't say much," he shrugged. "Why?"

"I don't want to make her uncomfortable."

"I am sure everything will be fine," he assured me. "I wouldn't have invited you both if I thought there would some kind of trouble."

"I promise I would never cause trouble at any of your parties," I squeezed his shoulder. "Especially your engagement party, John. And definitely not with her. She has been through enough."

He sucked in a deep breath. "She asked about you."

My jaw clenched as my head moved back and forth. "Why?"

"She just wanted to know how you were doing," sadness stole his features. "She asked about your sobriety too."

I shake my head, running a hand through my hair. "I miss her, you know?"

"She misses you too, kid," he sighs. "But there is a lot of tragedy there, and both of you needed time apart to realize how much you need one another."

"She doesn't want me," I winced. "Not anymore."

"She will always love you, Kinnick."

"I just wish she knew what I felt for her was real," I looked up at him. "She thinks I didn't love her."

"She knows," he smiled at me. "I know she knows."

I sucked in a deep breath. "Good because for whatever reason, I hope it brings her back to me."

"And what if it doesn't?" He shrugged. "Honestly, what if it doesn't?"

"I'll spend the rest of my life making sure she gets everything she wants in the world," my teeth clashed. "All I hope is that she finds somebody who makes her happy to wake up in the morning, even if that person isn't me."

Chapter 4

Whenever I spread the pages of my favorite novels, I wondered what it would be like to live in a castle. Would I be the one to wake up and look off of my balcony to see pastures of green and lakes of blue? Or would I be the boy from the wrong side of the tracks dressed in rags, pursuing the king's daughter? It made me think of Bo and how careless I was to Seth's wishes. If he thought the walls of a castle would keep up apart, I would burn his kingdom down. But that isn't something we have to worry about anymore. The princess doesn't want me because she finally realized the boy dressed in rags had absolutely nothing to offer her other than heartbreak.

It made me wonder what it would be like to chase her down the stone hallways and watch as her curly hair floated behind her. Would she look back at me with a smile on her face as she continued to play with my heart? Or would she let me carry her in my arms to her room as she told me to be quiet over two a.m kisses and early morning laughter?

Even if it were a fling, I'd let her break my heart over and over again as long as she promised to come back and do it again. I would do anything to have her by my side as I walked up the stone pathway to the palace John rented out. To watch the summer breeze drift by and catch the ends of her hair would be a sight to see. I wondered what she would wear. Would her hand be in mine? Would she steal kisses from my lips and turn a short walk into a twenty-minutes of nothing but blissful memories?

My eyes fluttered shut as I listened to the leaves rustling around me. With every step, I drew closer toward the building in front of me. I expected nothing less than royalty from John. The golden lights shined under every window, bringing a glow to the sky around it. And I started thinking about her reaction. Did she stare in amazement, or were her caramel eyes on the ground?

When I stepped inside to see the marble staircase John told me to walk up, I kept thinking about the curly-haired girl and how I planned on giving her everything she wanted. She wanted to dance in ballrooms wearing expensive dresses like they talked about in novels and go to the Orpheum dressed to her finest and listen to classical music. So, I knew her blood spiked when she saw the golden railing twisted into designs and how quickly she raced up the stairs even if she wanted to take things slow. I could practically see it so clearly my heart ached that it wasn't real.

The pad of my thumb ran over the letters on my wrist as my heart started to race. I haven't seen her in two years, and what happens when I do? How do I carry on with the party when my eyes meet hers, and I have to pretend like it means nothing?

I stepped through the corridor of the dimly lit room, staring at the lights strung across the ceiling. It looked like a night full of stars scattered above me. It brought a glow to the room, illuminating the wooden flooring. Being in the city had its perks - I could see every golden building from the floor-to-ceiling windows making up most of the room.

The glasses of champagne stacked on top of one another made a mountain of drinks, waiting for guests to take one. As they bubbled under the light, I caught sight of women in their nicest diamonds and men dressed in their finest suits. Something about this made me feel more like the boy from the side of the tracks than I did a member of John's family. I was starting to feel like I didn't belong here.

Just as I began to turn away to find John, a familiar burst of laughter stopped me in my tracks. I felt my chest tighten as my eyes immediately found the curly-haired girl I haven't seen in over two years. On top of her head sat a bun of ringlets; a few coils fell to frame her face. Her hair couldn't hide her glowing skin and her illuminating cheekbones.

It was as if the sun dropped from the sky to kiss her skin. It made the stars look like they weren't shining and the moon look like a joke. A deep breath of air pushed through my nose as the adoration sparkling in her caramel eyes as she stared up at John. My shoulders slumped just as my eyes began to burn. She had an aura that I never saw when she was around me, and I realized this is what genuine happiness looked like on her. And here I swore she couldn't get more beautiful.

I stood underneath the corridor, taking a few extra moments to look at the dress she chose to wear. The thin straps hung on her shoulders, and the front hung even lower on her chest. My eyes trailed over the long slit trailing up her leg where the material failed to meet, and that is when I saw the scar on her hip hiding underneath a strap of diamonds. The body chain hanging on her thigh glistened in the dim lighting, bringing attention to her golden brown thighs.

Just as tears began to well in my eyes, her head turned to look around the ballroom before she saw me amongst the crowd of strangers. I felt my heartbeat stop and accelerate all at once. And I couldn't tell if my heart was stopping or cracking as it shed from the darkness her light brought me.

When she couldn't break her gaze, I noticed the emotions welling in her eyes. The gloss hazed over her vision, dimming her glow. And as much as I wanted to stand there and pick out all of the changes I noticed about her, I didn't want to cause her any more pain. So, I walked away.

"Kinnick?" A soft voice called out to me.

I turned around to see Rosie, who came toward me in a low-hung red dress. "John said you were coming, I was wondering when you would show."

A smile tugged at my lips as I stared down at the woman pulling me into a hug. "How are you, Rosie?"

"A little tipsy," she chuckled as I kissed the top of her head. "How about you come inside? I can get you something to drink."

"I don't drink anymore," I shake my head.

"Not even punch?" She stared up at me with a bright smile. "It isn't spiked - I swear it."

My head moved up and down. "Very well. I guess I could let you get me a drink."

Her arm hooked around mine. "Now, I know you saw Bo. And before you deny it, I saw the tears in your eyes. No one has ever made you cry before, Kinnick."

"I wasn't going to deny it," I shake my head. "I don't want to talk about it, though."

"Both of you are hilarious," she pulled me toward a table filled with glasses and red punch. "I know you are both here for John, but don't act like you didn't want to see one another."

"She doesn't want to see me -"

"As a matter of fact, she has been asking a lot about you."

"Don't give me false hope," I grumbled. "I don't need that."

"False hope?" She snorted. "Stop being so stupid."

I stared down at the girl with her brown hair tied in a braided crown. "Someone is a little more than tipsy."

"Tipsy enough to think your friend Trevor is a little cute," she nodded in his direction with a smirk on her face. "Is he still single?"

"Yes," my eyes narrowed at her. "But nothing will happen between you two, do you understand me?"

She rolled her eyes, smacking my chest. "Oh, shut up. That is my brother's job to play protective dickhead."

"He isn't good for you, Rosie."

"That isn't your opinion to have," she sassed me back. "Plus, if all I am looking for is a one-night stand, it can't be that bad, right?"

I shake my head, rubbing my palm over my face. "Jesus, you are practically my little sister. I don't want to hear that."

A sly smile pulled across her lips. "Come dance with me, Kinnick Carson. Twirl me around the ballroom and tell me how beautiful I look."

"Yes, ma'am," I cleared my throat as her hand slipped into mine.

My fingers curled around her waist, steadying her in front of me as I slowly moved us back and forth. "Did I tell you how beautiful you look?"

"No," she tilted her head back to stare up at me. "Say it again."

A chuckle left my lips as I stared around the ballroom. "You look absolutely stunning, Rosie."

"How do you know if you haven't looked at me once this whole time?"

My chin tilted down as my eyes met hers. "I don't have to. You always look beautiful."

"What a charmer," she teased. "So, tell me how you have been."

"I don't want to talk about me," I pushed her away, twirling her in front of me. "Let's talk about you instead."

A string of giggles fell from her lips as I pulled her back into my chest. "Why would I do that when you are so much more interesting?"

"Me, interesting?"

"You are Kinnick Carson," her thumb rubbed across my suit. "What about you isn't interesting?"

I snorted. "All of it."

"Whatever," she sighed. "Tell me what I have to do to get his attention."

"Whose?" I furrowed my eyebrows in disbelief.

"Trevor's."

My head started moving back and forth. "Rosie, I told you -"

"He doesn't seem like the kind of man who makes the first move," she ignored me. "I guess I'll have to do it myself."

Before I could stop her, she broke free from my grasp. "Rosie!"

She flipped her straight hair over her bare shoulder, looking back at me as she dropped a wink. I sighed in frustration as she turned around without so much as another word. As she approached Trevor, I thought of ways to stop her. It wasn't that Trevor wouldn't treat her right because I would beat his fucking ass if he didn't, but Rosie wasn't grown enough for relationships yet. It just wasn't time. I feared it never would be.

"This isn't going to end well."

My head snapped to see Miles standing next to me, staring ahead at Rosie as she placed her hand on Trevor's shoulder. "No, it isn't."

"Does John know?"

I shake my head, staring at the side of his face. "I am sorry for what happened last week."

"I don't need your apology," his head moved back and forth. "But if you threaten Christina again, I promise it will be the last time you do it."

"Fair enough," I shrugged. "Where is she anyway?"

"Somewhere around here, helping a tipsy Bo stay on her feet."

"Bo is drunk?"

A smile cracked on his lips. "She is something else when she is intoxicated."

"Is she riding home with you?"

"I wouldn't let her ride with anybody else."

"And you will you keep her safe for me?"

"Of course," he nodded. "I made a promise to both of you."

"How is she doing? Honestly."

He turned to look at me with sorrow in his eyes. "Honestly? I don't know, Kinnick. After what happened between you two, she barely speaks to any of us. That little relationship she has with Luke is nothing. He thinks they are dating, but she only invites him to her room when she needs a distraction -"

"And after the accident, she started drinking. She thinks I don't know, but I smell it in her coffee. It lingers on her breath in the morning. Sometimes I can smell it on her clothes. Either way, I couldn't look you in the eye and tell you how she feels because I have no idea."

"I wish none of this shit ever happened," I squeezed my eyes shut. "I wish I could take it all away."

"Kinnick -"

"I am going to step outside," I cleared my throat as I patted his shoulder. "I'll be back soon."

"Are you going to be okay by yourself?"

Just as I walked away, my shoulders tipped upward. I wasn't sure. How could I answer his question if I didn't know the answer myself? Just before I slipped away from the ballroom, I caught sight of the curly-haired girl dancing with Chrissy. And I didn't want to be the reason the smile fell from her lips again. I was what started her whole world burning.

Chapter 5

My fingertips danced along the edges of my half-empty glass of champagne, and I hadn't taken a sip, but as I watched the curly-haired girl twirl around the ballroom, I thought about it. As my fingers continued moving circles around the four ounces of bubbling temptation, I lifted my eyes from the golden rim to see a bright smile on the face of the only woman I could ever love. As if I hadn't fallen for her the night of that party all of those years ago, I found myself dangling my feet over the edge of the walls she built, ready to fall deeper in love with her.

She stood in front of whoever was lucky enough to be in her presence, smiling with such prominent dimples I knew her cheeks hurt. When I leaned back into the chair, I pulled into the corner so she wouldn't see me; I watched her hand slip into someone else's. My heart nearly stopped at the sight of her fingers curling around Trevor's as he slowly spun her around.

And I couldn't blame him. After what I did, I couldn't blame him for going after that curly-haired girl the second he had the chance to. From the first time he met her in the cafeteria, I knew he had something for her. Now, he is pursuing the person my heart beats for, and I couldn't say a word. I couldn't even be the slightest bit upset.

My head moved back and forth with resilience, but the lump in my throat told me that it was okay to want to forget every now and then. I sucked in a deep breath before lifting the champagne glass a little higher. As I brought the rim to my lips, I felt the liquid scratch at my throat on the way down. It tasted like my first Thanksgiving with Bo when we shared the tub and how she promised to love me forever over champagne kisses and Sour Patch Kids.

As I brought the glass down from my lips, I stared at the droplets of what used to be a four-ounce fill of champagne, and it didn't take long for the torment to begin. My chair screeched loud enough for me to hear, but as I slammed my glass on the table, I wasn't seeing if anybody else did. My fingertips curled around the collar of my button-up, tugging until I heard rips and felt relief.

I shoved through the balcony doors, feeling the immediate relief of fresh air hitting my face as I stepped into the midnight atmosphere. The stillness sounded like loneliness, and the loneliness felt anguishing. My fingers ran through my hair as I leaned forward on the stone railing in front of me. My eyes burn with fiery tears, but I wouldn't let these embers hit the ground. I can't start another fire. I refuse to be the reason someone gets burned again.

Just as I turned around to leave, I reached for the door before it came flying toward me. My hand reached up to stop it from hitting me as someone crashed into my chest. Fingers curled around my suit as I stabled us both. As I began to apologize, I felt my heart relentlessly hitting my chest as it begged to get back to her.

"Bo," her name left my lips in a whisper, gone with the wind.

Her caramel eyes were widened. "I am sorry -"

"It's okay," my fingers fell away from her arm as I stepped away. "I was just leaving."

"I should have watched where I was going," she stuttered. "I am really drunk right now."

My head moved up and down as I tried to stare at anything but her. "Don't worry about it."

"You aren't going to scold me for drinking too much?"

I could practically smell the alcohol on her lips, but I started to shake my head. "No."

"Well, that is a first -"

Her lips started moving, and words fell from her lips, reminding me of everything I did wrong while trying to love her. Maybe I shouldn't have raised my voice every time she didn't want to tell me something. I could justify my actions, but making her cry was never justifiable.

Her confessions started my whole world hurting, and it made me realize I didn't deserve a second chance. Perhaps I should have loved her more. I should have held her tighter when the tears started to fall and soothed her when she felt scared. My hands should have made her feel safe and given her a shield of protection. I should have paid closer attention to what she smiled at and how her sleepy smile was more real than the one she gave me at two in the afternoon.

I should have loved her better. I should have done a million things and making sure she knew it should have been my first priority. Now I am standing in front of the woman I wanted a future with, but I realized all I have is memories of our past because we will never be present.

"Bo," I interrupted with my eyes closed as my heart continued to race. "Please."

And when her talking continued, my voice raised to cut hers out. "Bo."

Her lips parted as she stared at me with eyes that continued to grow more with despair. "Whatever you have to say, I don't want to hear it."

"Five minutes," I begged. "Just five minutes."

She turned to look at me with a stray tear trailing down her cheek, slowly running over her ruby red lips. "I can't do this again."

"All I ask for is five minutes," I pleaded as I stared down at her. "Just five minutes and you'll never have to see me again, Bo."

Her eyes squeezed shut, pushing out a few more tears. "What do you want from me, Kinnick? What is there left to say?"

"I have something to say. You just have to hear it," my vision blurred. "I have made a lot of mistakes in my life, but you were never one of them. I know you think my lips don't speak the truth, but I could never lie to you. I know my promises don't mean shit to you anymore, but one last time, I just want to promise you this; I will always look out for you, Bo. As long as I breathe, no harm will ever come your way. And everything you want in this world, I'll be there to make sure you get it -"

"One day, you are going to find somebody who treats you better than I did. They will hand you the galaxy when all I did was try to give you the world. And when you find them, you will forget about the pain I caused you. One day, you won't remember me, and only then will you know what true happiness feels like -"

"I am sorry for the pain I caused you, but after you are finished getting everything you want in this world, I promise to walk away. I'll leave everything we had behind because I know you want to live in a world that doesn't have me in it."

Her head snapped up to look at me. "What are you talking about?"

"My heart is yours, Boston Bennett," I wiped a tear from my eye before it fell. "It beats for nobody else."

"Kinnick -"

I stepped forward, pressing a gentle kiss to the top of her head as a sob broke from her lips. "I will always love you."

The pad of my thumb brushed over the cut on her cheek, clenching my jaw as I stared at the bruise under her makeup. Before I could start pressing her for answers, I turned away. The pain in my chest didn't stop me as her cries got louder. She didn't call out for me, so I didn't stop putting distance between us. And as I turned down the stairwell, I didn't look back. I couldn't. If I did, there was no promising I wouldn't go back to comfort her. And I couldn't do that to her. So, I did what I have been doing a lot since she left, walking away.

Chapter 6

My hand extended in front of me to shut off the ringing phone beside me, and the next thing I knew was glass shattering on the ground next to where I fell asleep. The sound cut through my head, piercing me with pain that pounded through my veins and made my eyes ache as they blinked open. When I found myself staring down at the familiar black sheets, I shoved away from the mattress below me.

Before I could slip away from the bed, I noticed the broken bottle of whiskey on the ground. A heavy sigh left my lips as I stared down at the mess, realizing I had drank it all. My feet planted firmly on the ground as I dropped my head into my hands, and all I could do was remind myself how badly I continued to fuck up.

It wasn't as hard to pick myself up from the bed, but how to make it from here to the door without seeing any of her stuff lying around the apartment. Everything remained the same. After the truth came out, I haven't been back here. The last night we shared together felt like the start of forever, but it was the beginning of an end. A tragic fucking ending.

I could never ask her to clean any of it up. From the shirts she stranded on the floor to the hair products all over the bathroom sink, I would never offer her the chance to get any of them back. Because if she erased every trace of the mark she left on my apartment, she would erase herself from me, and I needed something to prove it was all real - something to prove that she was real.

When my phone started ringing, I nearly found myself aching to throw it, but instead of letting the pain consume me, I slid the answer button across the screen. "What?"

"Kid?" John's soothing voice came through. "I didn't see you last night. So, I was calling to make sure you were okay."

"I am sorry I didn't stay longer," I rubbed my head as the throbbing continued to knock at my temple.

"I wasn't calling to express my sadness about your absence; I was calling to make sure you made it home safely and that you are doing okay."

"I am doing okay," I mumbled as I stared down at the broken glass on the floor. "Everything is fine."

A heavy sigh came from the other end. "I am always here if you need me."

"Congratulations, John," I kept my voice low as the guilt of ruining months of sobriety ate away at me. "I'll talk to you tomorrow."

"I love you, kid."

Without saying another word, I ended the phone call. I could never bring myself to say those three words to him. He considered himself my father, but I could never call him dad. The man who held that title was sitting in a prison cell, rotting away from the traces of abuse he left on my body. And as much as I despise that man, I stare down at the broken bottles on the floor, wondering if I am turning out to be just like him.

My hands never hurt a woman or scarred a child, but my criminal record says I have an issue with fighting. He used to drown in alcohol, but somehow I was the only one suffocating. Nowadays, I would drink my old man under the table. His alcohol levels could never reach mine, and that was something he would have been proud of. But how is it that I am turning out to be the man I hated the most in this world?

Every morning, I wake up wondering how to avoid the mirror. What if I can't stand the person staring back at me? What if I look in the mirror and I see my father? Because now I am alone, as is he, and I am trying to figure out what makes us any different.

Dizziness swept over me as I stood to my feet, but I could care less about the pain pounding in my head and the glass on the floor; I moved toward the duffle bag I hadn't touched in over a year. I slung the strap over my shoulder before moving toward the elevator doors. My eyes tried to stay focused on whatever was in front of me, afraid that if they steered away, I'd see something I didn't want to. And I don't know how I made it, but suddenly, I was in the elevator.

The effects of alcohol still swept over me in waves, making me nauseous with the slow movements. With the rain falling down upon me, I walked through the empty streets with my hands secured tightly in my pockets. Somehow when the world was falling apart and I didn't have a place to call my own, I always knew of somewhere I could call my temporary home.

When a bright light came from the familiar building, my eyebrows furrowed in confusion. The harsh weather made it difficult to see, but I wasn't blind to the person walking around the gym. As I grew closer, I noticed the man standing inside. I pulled on the door handle, allowing the small bell above me to ding.

"Kid?" John looked up from his clipboard. "What are you doing here?"

My head moved back and forth as I pulled down my hood. "I couldn't sleep."

He stopped flipping through his papers to give his attention to me. "Are you okay? I can smell - you know what, never mind. Did you come here because you needed a friend or a distraction?"

My eyebrows furrowed as I stared at him. "Why does it matter?"

"Because either way, I want to help you find a solution."

I dropped my duffle bag, signaling to the gloves I hadn't touched since the day John called off my fight. "This is all I know, and I don't know if I am lost because I haven't had it or because I don't have her, and I need to figure it out."

"Then wrap your hands and put on your gloves. I'll be around if you want to get in the ring."

"I want to fight again, John," I said as he turned away.

His head moved back and forth as his back turned to me. "You aren't ready for that, Kinnick."

"Not ready? There isn't a person fighting today who could beat me, John."

He walked toward me, pointing toward the side of his head. "Mentally, you are somewhere else."

"John -"

"I am not training you."

"Why are you turning me down?"

"Because you don't have good intentions."

"I need to fight again," the muscles in my neck strained as I snapped. "What do I have if I don't have this? This is all I know!"

"You are drinking again," his voice stayed hard even when tears welled in his eyes. "I can smell the fucking whiskey, Kinnick. If you want this, you'll change."

"I tried -"

"No, you didn't try," he barked as a tear fell down his face. "You started to feel something again and couldn't allow yourself to, so you drowned it out."

"You think I don't feel?" My voice raised. "Why do you think I picked up a bottle in the first place? You started carrying around Naloxone to save me from overdosing. How many times does it have to happen for you to realize I don't want to be saved anymore?"

"Kinnick -"

"I found somebody who made my fucking world spin. She helped me understand waking up in the morning didn't have to be so fucking hard. I never thought about escaping when I was around her. I stopped feeling the urge to use when I realized she got me higher than any drug. She made me crave sobriety. That curly-haired girl was my fucking redemption. She was my god damn reason -"

"And you think I am not capable of feeling, but she made me a different person. I felt what it was like when she was here, and I felt everything shift when she walked away. How am I to live when the person who made me feel alive isn't around anymore? Because I am struggling, John. It is as if all of the oxygen in the world has slowly started to disappear. There is no air left to breathe, and I am not trying to save myself. I am losing the biggest fight right now, but it isn't worth trying to win anymore. At this point, I am ready to throw in the towel."

Chapter 7

The music blaring through my headphones made it difficult to focus, but I needed it that way. Whenever I needed to stop thinking, I would turn my music up so loud that I couldn't hear my own thoughts. As I placed another fifteen pounds onto the weight bar, my arms struggled to not falter. All I wanted was to work myself until I couldn't feel anything other than the ache of my muscles. Boxing was a distraction, and nobody needed it more than I did. That is why nobody ever beat me.

John came toward me with a stack of papers in his hand before dropping them on the ground before me. My eyebrows furrowed in confusion as he crossed his arms, waiting for me to pick up the documents he tossed at my feet. I slipped the headphones from my ears as I bent over to pick up contract. As I looked over the writing, I knew what this was, but I couldn't understand why John was showing it to me.

After what happened in the previous hours, he made it clear that he didn't want to train me. He said I wasn't in the right state of mind to fight, but now he is showing me a potential rematch with the man

I was supposed to meet in the ring two years ago. I sucked in a deep breath before holding up the paperwork.

"Why are you showing me this?"

He shrugged as he stared at the ground. It was as if he contemplated the past few hours in his office, wondering if he should show me the contract he had been sitting on for what seemed like a while. After what I said, he walked away. I could see the tears streaking down his face as he left me in the lobby. I could hear his office door slam after I yelled at him. Now he is here, trying to make conversation.

"If you want to fight, this is your guy," he looked up from the mats below us. "You don't have another option unless you want to start at the bottom again."

"Start at the bottom?"

"You disappeared," he reminded me. "Did you forget that it has been two years since you stepped into a ring? If you want to be the best, you have to fight the best. And since you forfeited the belt, it is on the lign."

"I didn't forfeit -"

"You didn't fight for it either."

My jaw clenched as I bit back the urge to snap back at him. "What do I have to do then?"

"He wants it in Vegas again, his hometown," he shrugged. "There is nothing else. You either fight him or you lose your career. Your choice."

"How long have you been sitting on this?"

"After he came here a few weeks ago."

My eyes blinked a few times. "He was here?"

"Yeah," he nodded. "He wanted to talk about the rematch. Like I said, if you want to fight the best, you have to take out the best."

"If you are asking, I already told you I wanted this."

He grabbed the paperwork from my hands, shaking his head as he sucked in a deep breath. I wasn't sure what he wanted me to say. It was as if he wanted to give me the option, but he didn't want me to take it. I wasn't sure what he was questioning anymore - me as a person or me as a fighter. Without saying another word, he walked away.

"Wait," I called out to him.

He cocked a brow. "What?"

"You don't believe in me anymore, do you?"

He sighed. "It isn't that I don't believe in you, Kinnick. I don't know how to train you like this."

"You did before."

"Because you had something to fight for," he snapped. "You are doing it to get yourself hurt, and I am not okay with that. It never had anything to do with not believing in you as a fighter. I don't trust your intentions, Kinnick."

My eyebrows furrowed as I let out a ragged breath. "What am I supposed to do?"

"Get help -"

"I am coming to you!" I exclaimed. "I am turning to you for help because you are always here for me!"

"It isn't enough, though," his head moved back and forth. "I blame myself for putting you around the constant influences. If it wasn't for me, you wouldn't be in this situation. So, I tried to turn you away. I didn't want to train you because I didn't want to be the reason you couldn't stay sober."

"John, it was never your fault -"

"I tried loving your harder but it was never enough to keep you sober."

I stood from the bench. "You were never the reason for any of this. There are things I can't get right with myself, but none of those ever had to do with you."

"I have practically raised you and I feel like I am still doing it all wrong."

"You've kept me alive."

"And you made it clear that you wanted me to stop doing it."

"But it was never because of you."

"You are blinded by how much you love her," his eyes welled with tears. "You can't see how much all of us that are still present are here for you despite everything that has happened. We still love you too, Kinnick."

"It is different, John," I sighed. "Everything she witnessed, all of the trouble I caused her, she fell in love with me regardless. Everyone had a choice to stay by my side -"

"No, we didn't," he interrupted me. "From the moment I met you, I knew I would follow you to the ends of the earth. I never had a choice, Kinnick. My whole life has been a series of wondering where you are at in the world and if you are doing okay. I knew I had to make sure if you were safe every night, even if I failed ninety percent of the time. Despite everything, I am still here. I still love you. You are still my kid."

Chapter 8

Every morning, I watched the surveillance footage. It wasn't that I worried Trevor couldn't do his job, but he wasn't the only person working for me. All of my employees knew I watched the cameras to make sure everyone was doing their job, and because of that, I never had to worry. Nothing ever changed. Most of it remained the same.

I leaned back into my chair, sipping from the mug of coffee as the video continued to play. My eyes looked over the paperwork Trevor turned into me. Numbers have been steadily rising. The increase in percentages made it clear that business was only getting better. The team I had made recommendations that could help us, and it was proving to work.

Before pushing away from my desk, my eyes caught movement from behind the bar that caught my attention. I felt my lips part as I stared at the curly-haired girl trying to pull Trevor away from his job. My friend turned to Dan before following Bo toward the spot everyone danced. A smile stretched across his face as she held his hand, twirling herself around.

My eyebrows furrowed as a heavy sigh left my lips. Without make-up covering her face, I could see the scar on her cheek through the shitty resolution of my camera. It made me wonder how much worst it would be to see her in person.

"Hey," my office door flew open, revealing Trevor. "Shit, was I interrupting something?"

I hit the spacebar on my keyboard, pausing the video. "No. What do you need?"

"Before you watch the footage from last night, I need to tell you -"

"I already saw her," I cleared my throat. "Don't worry about it."

His head moved up and down as he stared at the ground. There were things he was keeping to himself. My elbows rested on the desk as I leaned forward. I cocked an eyebrow, wondering what made him silent. I didn't need his pity, though. If he was worried about me being upset, he could stop.

"I am fine -"

"She is drinking really heavily," he blurted. "It got to the point where I had to stop serving her."

My head dropped into my hands as I raked my fingers through my hair. "What are you talking about?"

"She cannot sleep anymore," he sighed. "She doesn't want to go home anymore. Her law firm is trying to get more security, but since she won't say anything about who did it, they can't help her."

"What do you mean they can't help her? That doesn't mean anything just because they don't know who did it -"

"It doesn't matter, she is scared," he snapped. "No amount of security is going to heal that."

"Why can she come to you guys, but she won't see me? She knows I can protect her -"

"Because this isn't about you."

"I never said it was -"

"She came to us because we are the closest thing she has to normal," he stated. "She doesn't have a family anymore, Kinnick. And when she didn't have anybody before, we were there for her. We are all she knows."

"Miles lives with her -"

"You killed her mom," he pointed at me. "We didn't say anything about it. There is a massive difference between those two statements. It is beside the point anyway. She is terrified of whoever it is that hurt her, and for whatever reason she has came to us for it."

"Has she told you anything?"

"Other than a few occasional things, no."

"Like what?"

He motioned toward his cheek. "The cut on her cheek, she said the man had hit her hard enough to fracture the bone -"

My breath hitched as I sucked in the air. The desk in front of me nearly tipped as I shoved away from it, standing to my feet. Who would want to hurt my Bo? Her whole life has been a series of kindness and being treated poorly. I couldn't understand why anybody would want to cause her pain.

"It is a hairline fracture," he continued cautiously. "She doesn't need to see a plastic surgeon. The doctor told her it should heal in less than four to six weeks. That is why the vessels in her right eye are broken."

"Someone hit her hard enough to fracture her cheekbone?"

"She is a small woman, Kinnick. I can't imagine that it would be hard -"

"What else did you find out?"

"The nerve running through her cheek is bruised," he cleared his throat. "So, parts of her face are numb. She said sometimes it is hard to drink because she cannot feel the corner of her lip."

I paced my office. "What does she need, Trevor?"

"She needs to feel safe -"

"Okay," I nodded. "Then you do whatever you have to. Just make sure it happens. If she needs somewhere to stay, I'll pay for it. Whatever it is, let me know. I'll take care of it."

"We need to do something about her job -"

"I'll hire someone for security," I shrugged. "Just don't tell her I am a part of any of this. I don't want her to say no."

He nodded. "For sure. I would never."

"Where is she staying when she is not at home?"

"I'll find out," he promised.

"Okay," I sat back down, rubbing my face.

Before he walked out, he turned back to me. "No matter what happens to her, she always asks about you."

When I found out about Warren, I wanted to do anything to kill him. Whatever I could do to prove to her that he would never hurt her again, I would do it. Yet, the whole time, I did what I could to suppress my anger. Every chance I had to put my hands on him, I would take it. Despite everything I did to him, she was still hurting. No matter how many times I hurt him, it would never help her heal. So, now I am trying to learn from those mistakes.

I couldn't be the Kinnick who went after the people who hurt her because I needed to feel better - it was never about me. I would start putting her first. Everything she needed, I would give it to her. In the end, she needed to be okay with herself. No one could heal her; she had to do it herself. I just had to support it, and I never did. So, now I am trying to change even if she doesn't see it.

Chapter 9

For two years, I spent more time keeping myself busy, so I didn't have to think about him. His absence didn't make falling asleep easier or stop the nightmares from coming more frequently. And I didn't realize how much I had changed until I was dancing around the ballroom tipsy off of expensive bottles of champagne with John.

When he invited me to his engagement party, I didn't ask if Kinnick was coming; I already knew. It led to questions about how the tattooed boxer was doing and how sobriety was treating him. My heart still resides with the blue-eyed man. After giving it to him, I wasn't sure if I could ever take it back.

Then he approached me at the party last night, and everything came rushing to the surface. I listened to his words, wondering how not to throw myself into his arms. How could I stand before him without saying how badly I have missed him since he has been away without thinking of my mom?

He wasn't the only reason I couldn't sleep. The pain in my cheek made me think about the man who visited me in my office, I couldn't get any rest. I struggled to feel safe in my home. If he could find me at my firm, I wondered if he would come looking for me there. So, my eyes won't close when my head hits the sheets.

It started with Luke - he would bury himself inside me whenever I needed relief. He thought I wanted a relationship with him - I wanted to forget about what happened to me. When he started getting attached, I stopped inviting him to my room and turned to alcohol. Now I am mixing it with my coffee to get through the day.

So, now I am turning to John. When he started talking about Kinnick, I sat back and listened as I imagined what it would feel like to see my boxer walk across the ring at this very moment. Except my boxer wasn't fighting anymore. It has been two years since he slipped into a pair of gloves. He hasn't raised his fists since he started to realize there was nothing left to fight for. It didn't sound like my Kinnick, but I wondered if it was because I am no longer his Bo.

The rain poured over John's car, pelting the glass with tiny droplets of water as they fell from the clouds above. As he drove past the front of the brick building, I could see a warm glowing light casting down on the damp sidewalk. My heart ached as the familiar boxing ring came into my view. Everything looked like a memory of yesterday. I shared so many memories with a blue-eyed boxer with many tattoos and twice as many secrets.

The trainer next to me told me about the nights he found Kinnick underneath the overflowing water in his bathtub. It was because he started drinking so heavily that he couldn't keep himself awake, but he was on the verge of alcohol poisoning and trying to save himself. John spoke so nonchalantly about it that I wondered how many times it happened, but I never asked.

And when he told me about the girls, the countless girls, I felt my heart drop. He told me how clear Kinnick made it when he slept around. He didn't want to replace me. He slept with these women to prove that he never could. But that didn't comfort me.

I didn't want to hear about the woman lucky enough to fall asleep in his bed underneath the satin sheets we used to share. On the same bed we used to tangle our bodies in. When the sun hit the bed just right in the morning, it caught his skin, and I remember wondering for the first time if this was love. Did she know how lucky she was, or did she not wake up early just to get a few moments to see him when he was most peaceful?

I wondered if they were gentle with him. Did they whisper that it was okay to take off his shirt because he was still ashamed of his scars? Or did he still have to get drunk every time he slept with someone because he still hasn't come to terms with his past? All I wanted to know was that they were kind to him.

"Do you want to go inside?"

I looked at the ring, wondering how not to think about him. "I don't know."

"Bo," he looked at me. "No matter what Kinnick has done, you will always be a big part of me. I have told you things before I couldn't trust with anybody else. Life has been better with you in it. I love you, kid."

I threw my arms around him. "I love you more, John."

"I am sorry for not telling you. I wish I could have, but it wasn't my place. I hope you understand that."

"I felt betrayed," I admitted. "I was embarrassed that everyone except for me knew."

"Nothing will ever be able to explain how sorry I am for that."

John opened the front door, allowing me to walk inside first. The warm weather made him open the windows and prop the door back. The breeze floating through made me think I could make it through without worrying about the possibility of something else happening. Before John could pull the pads from the closet, my phone started buzzing in my pocket.

"I'll be right back," I turned to John.

"Where are you going?"

"Outside."

"It is two in the morning."

"I'll be okay," I promised.

I pulled the hood over my head to keep me safe from the water. The rain was falling slowly. It hit the pavement softly, soothing my soul as I stepped into the night. I rubbed my temples, hoping to relieve the pressure in my head as I pulled my phone out.

The last thing I excepted was someone to be walking around in the middle of the night, but my shoulder slammed into someone. Before I could fall, a hand snaked around my waist, pulling me near the dark side of the street. I elbowed their ribs, making them lose grip on my body.

The last thing I excepted was someone walking around in the middle of the night, but my shoulder slammed into someone. Before I could fall, a hand snaked around my waist, pulling me near the dark side of the street. Fear flared through my body, making my limbs weak as I stumbled into the hold of a stranger.

"Bo," the familiar voice filled my ears.

My body betrayed me when it fell victim to his touch. I craved the heat radiating from his body. I let him consume me as his firm chest pressed against me. It reminded me how much I missed being in his hold, in his presence. Every muscle he trailed his fingers along ignited. I would always respond to him. He's the only one who knows my body inside and out.

The faint cigarette smell that lingered on him wasn't evident anymore. Alcohol didn't float off his breath. It was minty and sweet. The scent made you sigh with relief like you did when you stepped in the front door after being away from home after a long trip. As much as I wanted to push away, I was homesick.

His raspy voice hummed against me. "What are you doing out here by yourself?"

Chapter 10

My body shriveled up; my eyes squeezed at his tone. I melted in his hands like it was the first time hearing his voice. He has me wrapped around his finger. The worst part? He knows. What am I supposed to do when hearing him talk makes me feel safe? I felt untouchable around him. And I don't know what to do.

I let a sob rip through my throat from the absence in my chest. The feeling of being lost said I needed him to remind me who I was. I felt pathetic. The ache in my body, begging me to throw my arms around him, said to forgive him. How do I let go of the pain he caused me? How do I accept he was the reason for my mom's death and that he hid it from me? But I wondered if things would have been any different if he told me the second we met? Confusion made me ponder the thoughts.

"Hm?" He hummed into my ear.

I shoved him away with all the force I could muster up, yet his body didn't budge. The hood once casting a shadow over his face is now down. And I could see his face again. Those blue eyes I have come to love so much stared down at me with despair and regret.

"You are a fucking asshole!" My voice tore through my throat, making pain flare through the side of my face.

I cupped the side of my face as he frowned down at me. "Please, zip up your jacket. It is freezing."

I pointed at him as a thousand words begged to roll off my tongue, but nothing came out. So, a scream of frustration ripped through my throat instead. He did nothing but stand before me with remorse on his face, watching as I paced back and forth. And I hated it. I hated it all.

The resentment coursing through my veins has been there ever since the truth came out. Right now, it's growing more vital than ever. As I stared at his face and all of the times we spent together came rushing back. I felt my body going numb with irritability.

I pushed him back again, making him sigh. "Why?"

"Why?" I screamed, shoving him backward.

My fists continued to collide with his chest. It didn't hurt him. Nothing hurts him, but god, did I wish it did. I wanted him to hurt as much as I did. He stood there, letting me wail on him, without an expression on his face. I wanted a reaction. I wanted him to fight back. I wanted a fucking answer.

"Bo," he gripped my wrists. "Stop."

I struggled in his grip. His hold never faltered as I thrashed around. "Damn it, stop!"

"I missed you!" My voice cracked as it changed in pitch. "And I don't want to!"

His fingers curled around my forearms, pulling me into his chest despite my efforts to fight him off. And when my cheek pressed against his skin, I felt myself relaxing in his hold. Nothing about my life has felt right. I have been existing without feeling alive. Then his arms wrapped around me, and warmth spread through my body. I realized at that moment that I never wanted to be more alive than I do now.

"Why did you leave me on that balcony alone?"

His hands tightened on me. "You never asked me to stay."

"I never asked you to go either."

"Forgive me then," he pleaded. "All I ever wanted was for you to be happy."

"But I am not."

"Then what can I do for you?"

My hands pressed against his chest, putting distance between us. "Tell me none of it was real."

"What part?" He winced. "Because I am not going to look you in the eyes and say that what I felt wasn't real."

"Why?" My throat began to ache as I struggled to keep the lump at bay. "Just say it wasn't real. Just say that none of it meant anything to you."

"If it didn't mean anything to me, I wouldn't have approached you at the party last night," his eyes began to gloss over. "If I didn't love you, I wouldn't have called Miles to make sure you made it home safely! I wouldn't have came down here to make sure nothing happened to you while you were on your phone. I wouldn't be standing in front of you right now, hoping that I could say something that would make you come back home!"

"I don't want you to love me anymore."

"That is pretty fucking hard, Bo," he snapped. "Considering, before you, I didn't have a reason to wake up in the morning, I don't know how to do that."

"You did it before - do it again!"

"I have loved you since I saw you at the party that night!"

"You didn't know me!"

"I didn't have to," he choked. "I just knew when I saw you, my life would never be the same."

"You didn't even talk to me."

"Nothing in my life has scared me since my dad went to prison," he sucked in harsh breaths. "Except for you, Bo."

"Why?"

"How clear do I have to make it to you? I fucking love you!" He ran his fingers through his hair. "Every little thing you do gets me going! I never had to worry about any opponent I have ever stepped in the ring with, but the way you talk and hold yourself knocks me the fuck out."

I choked on a sob as he continued raising his voice at me. "What the fuck do I have to do to prove to you that I love you?"

"Walk away."

"Is that what you want?" He snapped. "You want me to act like this never happened? You never want to see me again?"

"Yes -"

"Then look me in my fucking eyes and tell me that yourself," his voice dropped lower. "Look at me and say that you never want to see me again, and I will walk away without hesitating."

"Just like that? Without protest?"

His jaw clenched before his lips parted. "Just like that."

And before I could say another word to him, John was calling out from the entrance of the alleyway. "Bo?"

My head snapped to look at him, but I could see Kinnick's hard eyes staring at the side of my face. "John."

"Is everything okay?" He asked as he approached us.

"You can't say it," Kinnick spoke regardless of John standing there. "Just fucking admit it."

"Kinnick," John snapped. "Stop."

"No, he is right," my eyes met the blue-eyed boxer's. "I can't say it. I still love you, but that doesn't mean I am going to fall at your feet, and come crawling back. It has taken you two years to say something to me, and it wasn't because you sought me out. You stumbled across me at a party. I don't trust you, Kinnick. And that is your problem. Not mine."

Chapter 11

There wasn't a question about why I followed them inside the gym, even if I knew she didn't want me around. I would go wherever Bo went, though. My back leaned against the chair as she tightened the strap of a new pair of gloves around her wrists. I wasn't sure what I loved more, the black color she chose to wear or the pink ones she used to have when we trained together. Either way, I couldn't keep my eyes off her as she threw punches at the pads on John's hands.

The broken vessels in her eye hadn't healed. Everything was still fresh. It made me wonder why John allowed her to be in the ring. If something happened, I would try to refrain myself. I think I could adequately breathe as long as I remembered she wanted this. The feeling coursing through my veins made it difficult to stare at her swollen cheek without wanting to interrogate her.

As much as she hated my staring, I continued to do it. People tend to stare at things they think are cute, and she happened to be pretty fucking cute. So, I would continue staring because I could lose my eyesight anyday. And while she stands in the ring, staring at the man in front of her as her head falls back with laughter, I am memorizing every part of her face as if that day would come tomorrow.

The bouncing of her body stopped as she clutched her stomach, expressing her happiness as John continued to say something that made her laugh. The curly-haired girl looked genuinely happy until you noticed the discoloration under her eyes. Her skin had started to lose its glow, and with every strike she made, I noticed she had grown weaker.

My arms crossed over one another, resting on my torso as my legs started to bounce. Just like when Warren came back around, there were significant changes I caught on to that she didn't want me to see. Out of everybody, she knew I would be the one to call her out. I cared about her, so I asked too many questions and continued asking until I got answers. Whoever hurt her made fear strike her body in a way it never had before.

It made my knuckles ache. The feeling coursing through my body made me worry about what I would do, even if I tried telling myself not to do something stupid. The chair scraped the ground as I stood up. I couldn't help the sound that made them halt their actions, but I couldn't sit there and stare at her without driving myself crazy.

I shoved through the bathroom door, running my fingers through my hair as I tried to breathe deeply. I splashed cold water over my face as I leaned over the sink. I couldn't scare her away, no matter how upset I was with what happened. She was already tip-toeing around me, and it made me wonder if she had heard about what happened with the man at the bar. And now I have to worry if she is scared of me because I don't want to live in a world where the girl I want to protect is wanted to be protected from me.

When my breathing calmed, I walked out to see Bo barely standing straight. My eyebrows furrowed in confusion as I watched her arms falter. John must have seen her drooping eyes as he instructed her to pay attention. He kept pushing her to hit him, and now I am starting to ask if he was going blind.

"John, can I talk to you?"

He turned to me, motioning between him and Bo. "I am busy. Can it wait?"

"Now," I snapped.

Before he stepped out of the ring, I could hear him mumble to Bo that I still had anger issues. It didn't upset me, but hearing her laughter made everything better. I could hear John's footsteps behind me as I walked toward his office, and the second we stepped inside, I couldn't stop myself from snapping at him.

"She is fucking tired!"

He furrowed his eyebrows. "Did you ask me to come in here just for that?"

I sucked in a deep breath, raking my fingers through my hair. "She is clearly exhausted! Can you not fucking see that?"

"Yes, I can," he rolled his eyes. "That is the point. She can't sleep, so I am trying to help her."

"By working her until she passes out?"

"Kinnick," he checked behind him to ensure she wasn't close. "She can't sleep anymore. You aren't there to keep the nightmares away. What am I supposed to do when she calls me in the middle of the night, asking for help?"

"If you hurt her," I seethe. "I will kill you."

He rolled his eyes again. "Whatever you say."

"I am serious."

"I am serious," he mocked. "My name is Kinnick, fear me."

"Fuck you," I shoved him backward.

A snort of laughter left his lips. "Fuck you, John. You are always so mean to me."

I shoved through the door as he followed behind me. "I am done with your shit."

When I stepped out of the hallway, I saw Bo sitting on the bench. A smile crossed her face as she stared down at her phone. I wondered if she was texting Luke, but what did he say to make her smile? I know the piece of shit; he never said anything funny. John called out to her, asking for help as he searched for something in the backroom.

"I'll get a ride home," Bo said as she grew closer.

Before I could look at her phone, I stepped away. John cocked his eyebrows in questioning as if he knew what I was doing, but he kept motioning to the girl his arms were wrapped around. I threw my hands up, wondering what the fuck he wanted me to do. And I suck at reading lips, but I swore he told me to give her a ride home.

She broke their hug before picking up her duffle bag and walking past me as if I didn't exist. John threw himself into the air, pointing toward the door with a red face as she slipped into the rainy night.

"What the fuck is your problem?" I bite.

"You aren't going to go after her?" The muscles in his neck strain. "You are an idiot if you let her walk away! Especially after what she told you."

Without second-guessing, I shoved through the door after her. My heart stopped as she stood in the same place I saw her for the first time since the party. Her eyes were focused on the phone in her hands as if she were waiting for her dad to pick her up again. I sucked in a deep breath and struggled to think of something to say.

"Something makes me think you are waiting for everyone to fall asleep so you can make it home safely."

She pivoted on her feet, staring at me with furrowed eyebrows. "Something like that."

"Is Chrissy coming to get you?"

"Uh - I think I'll get -"

"Do you want to get something to eat?"

Her eyes widened. "It is like three in the morning."

"Yeah," I shrugged. "I can take you to my bar."

"I need to take a shower," she cleared her throat. "And change."

"You have clothes at my place."

She sighed. "Kinnick, no."

"I'll make you dinner there if you prefer that."

"I don't want to go back there," she mumbled.

The pain felt like something snapping in my chest. "Okay."

"I'll go to the bar," she sighed.

"My truck is out back," I pointed behind me. "I left it here the other night."

She kept her distance as she trailed beside me. "Why?"

"I was drunk," I cleared my throat. "I didn't want to drive."

"I thought you weren't drinking anymore?"

My head moved back and forth. "I wasn't."

"Oh."

My fingers raked through my hair as the air grew uncomfortable. "How is work?"

"You want to talk about how work is going?"

"Well, I don't know," my hands started to shake. "What do you want to talk about?"

"I want to know why you asked me to go to Rosie's."

My eyes rolled out of disbelief. "Bo, I already told you."

"Well, I want to hear it again," she refused to open the passenger's side door. "What do you want from me, Kinnick?"

My elbow leaned against the car door as I avoided her gaze. I wasn't sure what she wanted me to say. There were so many things going through my mind that I couldn't figure out what to say first. I wasn't sure if she would actually want to hear any of it.

"Whatever," she mumbled before turning away. "I am not doing this."

"Are you serious?" I shut my car door as I walked around the truck. "Where are you going?"

"I am going to find a ride home," she continued walking away.

"You are leaving because I won't answer your question?"

"Yes!" She flipped around. "I want to know what your intentions are, is that wrong? I want to know what you want from me!"

"I want you!" I smacked the hood of my truck, making her stop walking. "I want you! It has always been you, Boston Bennett! I just want you. Now, get in the damn truck, and let me take you to get something to eat."

The curly-haired girl hesitated, but she came back to me. "I don't know why you are working so hard. It will never work out."

"But you are getting in my truck, so it makes me think you want to try," I turn over my engine. "And I am not giving up on you, Bo."

"I don't know why."

I wasn't sure how much more clear I had to make it. "Because my whole life I have trained to box, but you were the only thing worth fighting for."

Chapter 12

The curly-haired girl breathed down my neck as we walked through the empty bar. She stayed close through the dark hallways as if she thought someone would pop around the corner and scare her. I could feel the heat radiating from her body as I unlocked my office door. I flipped the switches, allowing light to fill the room as she awaited relief.

I wasn't oblivious to the breath she let out after the darkness was drowned out by the golden chandelier hanging above us. It wasn't that I had the answers to why her hands were shaking, but I didn't ask. She didn't want me to question her, and I wasn't in the place to do so. If she wanted me to know, she would tell me, or that is what I hope anyway.

Her curious eyes looked at the blanket sprawled out on the couch as if it made her confused. It was clear I was sleeping in my office most nights, but she didn't say a word as she followed me out of the room. I stepped behind the bar to turn the grill on as she walked around to find a seat.

The silence didn't feel uncomfortable, but it made me wonder if the whole night would be like this. I knew that I would sit in a room without us saying anything if that meant I got to sit with her, though. Anything with Bo is better than nothing at all. So, I settled for the silence and continued preparing the kitchen.

As I broke open the bag of chicken strips, I peeked around the corner to check on her. My lips parted as I watched her pull down the curls I loved so much from the bun she held them in. The chestnut coils fell down her back as I ached to run my fingers through them. She rested her cheek on her palm as her tired eyes looked at the screen of her phone.

"Do you want something to drink?"

Her head snapped up to look at me. "Uh - sure. Can I have a water?"

I scooped ice from the machine before dumping it into her glass. She watched as I pulled the hose over to her glass, letting the machine fill her cup with fresh water. I grabbed a yellow straw from the basket underneath the bar, popping it into her cup.

"Do you need anything else while that cooks?"

"How did you know what I wanted?"

"Well, every time we went out together, you only ordered chicken strips because it was the only meal you could eat with a lot of ranch."

My heart flipped as the corner of her lips tugged upward - not enough for a smile but enough for me to see. Her lips wrapped around her straw before I walked back into the kitchen. The oil popped, sending small droplets to splash against my skin as I dropped in the chicken. After a while, I got used to the pain.

As I moved the strainer around in the oil, she fidgeted around on the barstool. When the bread sizzled into a golden brown, I pulled it from the hot substance. Steam filled the air as I dropped the chicken into the baskets.

"So, are you training again?"

My eyebrows furrowed as she began making small talk. "Yeah."

"For a fight?"

I leaned against the doorway as I looked at the curly-haired girl. "I signed a contract last night to fight the same man I was supposed to meet in Vegas."

She went silent as her head moved up and down. "Tommy, right?"

"Yeah," I nodded. "I didn't think you would remember."

"I was supposed to go with you."

"I know," I clenched my jaw. "That's okay, though."

"I was watching that night," she cleared her throat. "I remember listening to my phone go off when everyone started posting about you being rushed to the hospital that night."

"Yeah, I have done a lot of stupid shit in my life."

"Was it my fault?" She swallowed harshly.

My lips parted in disbelief. "Why would it ever be your fault? I chose to take those drugs, Bo."

"I know you, Kinnick," she sighed. "When you don't know how to handle something, you turn to whatever gets rid of the pain the fastest. I was the reason you were taking drugs, though."

"I walked around the city with half of me, knowing the other half is somewhere else in this world trying to forget who I am," I admitted. "You made me feel whole, and when you left, I felt all of me go with you. Did I drink too much? Yes. Was I taking random drugs? Yes. Either way, I am the one who did both. It was never your fault for how I chose to forget."

She didn't say anything else, so I did. "Can you answer a question for me with complete honesty?"

Her eyes lifted from the bar. "Yes."

"Do you know who attacked you?"

A frown settled on her face as she kept her eyes on me. "I knew of him, but I don't know him."

"Do you feel comfortable telling me what happened?"

"After Marcus and I won our case, we went to celebrate at the bar across the street from my firm," she mumbled. "I went back to the firm when I couldn't find my phone. My office door was cracked open. At that moment, I was plastered, so I didn't question if I had locked it before we left. The second I walked through, I saw him standing at my desk. There was no getting away; he already had ahold of me before I could turn around. I tried fighting back to give myself time to run -"

Her voice cracked as tears welled in her eyes. "When I collided with the ground, I knew something had happened, but I couldn't feel the side of my face. Before registering everything, my hand reached up to touch my cheek. When I pulled them away, they were covered in blood. I could feel it pouring down my face."

"Why was he there, Bo?"

"He wanted me to send a message," she whimpered.

"To who?"

"I don't know," a sob broke through her lips. "I don't know. I am just scared."

Without hesitating, I came around the bar. She didn't protest as I wrapped my arms around her. She turned around on the barstool before throwing herself into my chest. I ran my fingers through her hair, trying to soothe her as she cried. The most I could do was be here for her, even if I wanted to be on the streets trying to find the man who hurt my girl.

"What do you need from me?" I murmured into her curls. "I will do whatever you need me to."

"I'll be okay."

"We both know that is a lie."

"It isn't your problem anymore," she pushed away from me, putting distance between our bodies.

"You were never a problem to begin with."

She inhaled deeply. "I am not feeling hungry anymore."

"Have you eaten all day today?"

"I'll be okay," she avoided my eyes.

"Do you want me to give you a ride back to your place?"

Her head moved up and down. "Please?"

"Of course," I cleared my throat. "Let me shut everything down."

"I am sorry all of this was for nothing."

"I will take anything I can get."

"Thank you, though," she murmured.

The corner of my lips tugged upward as I stared down at the curly-haired girl. "Anytime."

Chapter 13

My palms hit the cool surface of my white comforter as I stirred around the satin sheets. The golden light cast down on my face made me grow uncomfortable. It made sleeping difficult, but it was the first time I woke up to the morning sun and not a nightmare. My nose inhaled the scent of fresh linen as I closed my eyes gently. The muscles in my body felt relaxed, but my mind made my heart pound with tension.

I felt curiosity eating away at me as I looked down at the hoodie on my body. The black material felt soft against my bare skin. I brought the collar to my nose as I sucked in the comforting scent, and although I couldn't decipher what it was, it smelt like home. It smelt like Kinnick. It reminded me of our first hug and how I was consumed and captivated all at once.

Flashbacks of last night felt like a strobing light in my head. The memories were coming in spurts, but the faster they arrived, the more I could piece the story together. When he asked me to talk about what happened, I opened myself up to him. Yet, there was a mental blockage, and it stacked bricks in between us that made it difficult to talk. After screaming for help for so long, I realized he couldn't hear me through the retaining wall, so I stopped trying. I lost my voice.

It felt exhausting trusting Kinnick. With every brick I laid to conceal myself from him, he would smile at me, and I would knock them back down again. This dam of emotions was meant to keep me safe, but the walls I have built didn't pass code, and now the city is calling for an inspection.

Before deciding how everything made me feel, my eyes caught sight of a white envelope leaning against my lamp on the bedside table. My name was written in calligraphy across the center as if it had been waiting for me.

My fingers ran over the smooth surface before breaking open the seal. I furrowed my eyebrows in confusion as I pulled a Scooter's gift card from the envelope. The beating of my heart accelerated when a little white paper fell onto my lap. As I unfolded the note, I saw Kinnick's familiar handwriting etched in between the gray lines.

"By now, your stomach should be growling, and if it is, there is $100 loaded on your Scooter's gift card, so you can buy yourself as many blueberry muffins and strawberry vertigos you desire. But if you want actual food, breakfast is waiting for you at the bar. If you choose not to come, I will understand - Kinnick."

My eyes lifted from the letter as Luke came through my bedroom door. "Sorry, I wanted to make sure you made it home safely."

"It is okay," I folded the paper in my hands. "Did you need anything else?"

"I thought we could go out for lunch or something."

"Actually, I am meeting someone this morning."

"Who?"

I slid out of my bed as I searched for a clean towel. "An old friend, but I am going to take a shower. So, we'll have to figure something out another time."

Unlike other times I have spent in the shower, I rushed myself to get out. If this were any other day, I would spend hours underneath the warm water as I let it soothe the muscles in my aching body. Yet, I quickly dressed before stopping by Chrissy's room to see if she wanted to go with me.

"What are you up to?" I asked as I watched her paint her toenails.

"Nothing important; what's up?"

"I'm going out for breakfast if you want to join?"

"Duh!"

Chrissy told me it concerned her when I didn't come home last night. After discovering my new drinking habits, she worried that something had happened. To soothe her, I said I visited John at the gym. There wasn't an obligation to tell her about Kinnick. If I told her, she would ask how I felt as if my life had to be spread out on a sheet for everyone to understand. But when we stepped into the bar and saw Kinnick, she looked at me with concern.

Trevor greeted us as we sat at the bar. "You showed up."

The corner of my lips tugged upward. "Yes."

"There are cinnamon rolls in the oven," he slid two glasses toward us. "Homemade, by the way."

"Homemade?"

"I am quite the baker, miss Bennett."

"We will be the judge of that," I teased as I pulled a fifty from my wallet. "Here."

"For what?"

"Making homemade cinnamon rolls, even when they aren't on the menu."

"Kinnick won't let you pay -"

"Then keep it as a tip."

He cautiously moved away from us as he walked toward the cash register. I watched Kinnick ask him what he was doing as he placed the money inside the drawer. Trevor pointed down toward me, making my gaze drop as I told Chrissy to brace herself. She furrowed her eyes in confusion.

Kinnick smacked the fifty-dollar bill down on the table. "Take it back."

"Do not talk to me in that tone."

"Then take your money."

"Or what?"

He snatched my wallet off of the counter, shoving the cash inside. "Kinnick!"

"You don't pay here, understood?"

"I am a customer."

"A customer that doesn't pay," he tossed my wallet onto the bar. "Are we done here?"

"I don't know. Are you going to accept my money?"

He turned to Trevor. "If you take money from her, I will break your fingers."

"But she threatened me."

"I am threatening you."

"She is -"

"I don't care. I am your boss."

Trevor looked at me with worry. "Trevor, I will never come back here."

His green eyes looked back at Kinnick. "I don't know what to do."

"Boston," Kinnick snapped. "You are not paying. End of story."

"I am taking my service elsewhere."

"What other bar is going to give you endless supplies of ranch?"

I looked at his blue eyes, narrowing in on him. "You are a jerk."

Before he walked away, he dropped a napkin in front of me. My eyebrows furrowed as I read the sloppy handwriting. "You look beautiful today - your Augustus Waters."

Chapter 14

After Kinnick left me a gift card for Scooters, I continuously bought coffee throughout the day for work. Evan asked me to revisit the paperwork ruined during the attack, but every time I sit down, flashbacks of what happened play through my mind every time I sit down. I couldn't decipher if my hands were shaking from the caffeine or the fear I felt.

So, I reorganized my office. Then I didn't like where my filing cabinet sat, so I changed it again and again, and now it is two in the morning, and I am still figuring out the things I don't like. The candles burning on my window seal lit up the room. The flickering glow cast a glare on the wooden floor, but I adored how the moonlight shined on the white walls. Something felt calming about sitting in a dark room lit up by the moon and golden candles despite everything that happened.

A slight knock came from my opened door, catching me off guard. My body jolted forward as I looked up to see a stranger standing in my doorway. His tall stature gave me goosebumps, but I never attempted to leave. I felt frozen again.

"Can I help you?"

A smile twisted on his lips. "I am the new security officer. I am just making my rounds."

"I wasn't aware we hired anybody."

"Oh," he reached for a badge on his hip. "This is my identification card. Evan said I would be getting an official badge in a week, but Marcus said that really means in a few months."

A chuckle spewed past my lips as the muscles in my shoulders relaxed. "Well, it is nice to meet you - sorry I didn't catch your name."

"Brian," he blurted. "I should have started with my name."

His pink-tinted cheeks made me grin. "It's okay."

"You are Boston, right?"

"Yes," I nodded.

"Well, it was nice meeting you," he smiled. "As long as I am around, I can assure that nothing will happen to you."

My heart swelled because I remembered when Kinnick said that to me and how I still only believe it when it falls from his lips. Now my trust is in the hands of a new security officer. Brian gave me one last farewell before disappearing around the corner. I looked at the clock on my phone, noticing thirteen hours had passed.

When I told Brian that I was leaving, he walked me to my car. He even stayed to make sure my car started, which it didn't. Now we are back inside. As he sat at the front desk, I tried calling anybody who would answer, but their phones went straight to voicemail. My fingers trailed over a familiar number, but my phone had already started to dial it before I could protest.

"Bo?"

I sucked in a deep breath as I struggled to stay calm. "Kinnick? I am sorry. I didn't mean to call you. I am sorry if you were asleep. It was an accident -"

"Slow down," his raspy voice soothed me in the same way it made me want to cry. "Are you okay?"

I blew a breath through my lips. "I'll be fine."

"Where are you?"

My head fell into my palm. "Work."

"It is almost two in the morning," I could practically hear his eyebrows furrowing. "Why are you still at work?"

"I didn't want to go home," I sighed. "Now I can't go home -"

"Why can't you go home?"

"My car won't start," my lip quivered. "I will call a cab. It will be fine -"

I heard the elevator ding. "I am on my way."

The feeling of guilt rushing through my body made me suffocate. I didn't want to be why he woke from a peaceful slumber. I, of all people, know what it is like to lose sleep. I didn't want to be the person to take that from him. He didn't seem to care.

Brian refused to leave, but I promised Kinnick would be here soon, and I wouldn't need him to stay. Plus, it was late. He needed his sleep too. Now, I am sitting outside, listening to Kinnick talk.

I missed hearing how his voice changed when he woke up from a deep sleep. It still sent shivers down my spine to hear it. No matter what happened, my body always reacted to him. The butterflies were still flapping their wings, creating a beautifully chaotic swarm of warmth in my stomach.

When I tried hanging up, he insisted on staying on the phone. He didn't want something to happen. I know he doesn't believe him being on the phone would stop someone from hurting me if they wanted to, but staying on the phone assured him I was okay. So, I did whatever soothed his worrying mind. He deserved that after everything.

I listened to his truck start as he asked me about my day. The conversation was awkward, but he was the only person I wanted to talk to. My feet stretched out in front of me as I sat on the stairs outside, taking in the warm breeze as it drifted by. He could hear the wind as it blew through the phone. I know how badly he wanted to tell me to go inside. He didn't. He just asked me to be aware of my surroundings.

Things felt normal even though they felt awkward. Talking to him was familiar. It was coming home after spending a week away. During the time we talked, everything came rushing back. We were together again, and I wasn't heavily drinking to get my mind off of things. I was coming home to the man I loved more than anything in this world.

"I am close," his raspy voice assured me. "Are you still okay?"

I looked at the stars as I leaned back on the concrete stairs. "Better than ever."

Lights flashed over my body. My heart picked up as I looked at the vehicle. "It's me, Bo. You're okay."

He stayed on the phone even when his body exited the car. I stood up from the stairs, and before he could prepare himself, I ran down to him. I threw my body towards him, wrapping him in my arms. His touch was hesitant, as if he would break me by simply laying his hands on me. But when he did, the world fell away.

"What is wrong, Bo?"

My face dug deeper into his chest. "Just hold me, please."

I let out a sigh as his arms wrapped around my lower back. He circled me into his chest, pulling me tighter to him. As his face brushed my neck, I could feel his lips moving against my skin.

"What happened, baby?"

My head moved back and forth as I fell victim to his touch. "Not right now, please."

"Come on," he nudged me. "Let me get you home."

Chapter 15

My fingers tightened around the steering wheel as I drove down the street without a destination. She didn't say a word, but I didn't need her to. Brian told me nobody would answer her phone calls, and when he came knocking, she promised everything was okay.

The curly-haired girl next to me didn't know I threatened her boss into hiring a security guard for their firm at my recommendation. Now I never have to worry about Bo being attacked in her office again. It has been difficult to sleep without knowing she was lying next to me. No one else could keep her safe. Not like I could.

So, I asked her why she called me. Was it a mistake, or did she get embarrassed? I wanted to see if I was the first person or the last on her mind. It didn't matter either way as long as she thought about me. All I wanted to hear was that after everything, she still thought about me. Even if it was something stupid, I wanted to know she couldn't forget about me.

"I didn't mean to -"

"But how did you click on my name?"

Her face turned to stare outside. "I always scroll past your name."

My heart started to race. "Why?"

"Sometimes, I just wonder what you are doing."

The aching in my chest told me not to look at her again, but I did anyway. I needed to torture myself. I craved to see her button nose and the hint of kissable pink on her lips. After the hug she gave me, I wanted to know if she was looking too. Did she miss me as severely as I missed her?

When we pulled up to a red light, I eased on the brake, and I stole a glance in her direction. She had her head leaning on the window, staring at the buildings in front of us. Her sweet scent disrupted the cigarette smell brewing in my car.

I spent months chain-smoking to get rid of her fragrance. Dust built up on the dash, and alcohol bottles piled on the floor. I would do anything to hide traces of Bo until I realized it was never going away. So, I stopped driving and started walking wherever I needed to go.

"Why didn't you call Luke?"

"I did."

"And?"

"And nothing," her voice cracked. "He never answered."

I gripped the steering wheel tighter. "He didn't answer you?"

"Yes," she snapped. "Is that what you want to hear? Did you want to hear that he doesn't care if I am safe or even answer when I call?"

My jaw clenched as my teeth ground against one another. "What makes you think that?"

"Don't act like you don't," her hand wiped a tear from her face so quickly I almost didn't notice it.

Her small hands gripped her seatbelt as I pulled my truck over to the side of the road. "Are you fucking kidding me?"

"Kinnick -"

I threw my truck into park, "I wanted to hear you're happy and life has been better since I left. I wanted you to tell me you and Luke are in love and that he's everything you've ever wanted. Even if you aren't dating, I wanted you to find somebody else. I wanted you to forget about me and realize shit is easier without me."

"Kinnick -"

"I'm sorry you couldn't introduce me to your dad for the first time over dinner. I'm sorry I couldn't have the awkward dad talk with him. I wanted nothing more than to pick you up for a date and be threatened to bring you home before ten."

"Please stop."

"I'm sorry I got behind the wheel that night drunk," my voice broke, and tears pooled in my eyes. "I'm sorry your mom couldn't see you graduate and celebrate you winning your first case. I'm sorry she couldn't help you decorate your first apartment. I fucked up!"

"But if you think for one second that I would want the worst for you," my voice dropped. "Then you have lost your fucking mind because I love you, Boston. I will go to the ends of this earth to make sure you are safe and that you get everything you deserve in life."

Her face fell into her hands as sobs left her lips, so I continued talking. "I can see the lack of sleep on your face. Do you want to come back to the apartment? You can sleep for as long as you need to. I'll take care of you and make sure you are safe. I'll do whatever I have to so you can rest -"

"Please," she whimpered. "Take me home."

My hand wiped over my face as I nodded, feeling the dam of emotions rushing over me in waves. "Yeah, whatever you want."

"I just want to go with you," she begged. "Take me home with you, please."

I didn't think twice when I pulled a u-turn. My truck's tires shot dust onto the main road as I moved in the direction of our apartment. I wasn't sure what would happen when tomorrow came or when Luke called her, but she told me home was with me, and that was all that mattered.

She wasn't awake to see me taking a long way. Bo wasn't going to question why I went down random streets so she could stay asleep a bit longer. The moment I tried to move her, I knew she would wake up. So, I stayed on the road until my eyes began to falter. I would do whatever I had to do to ensure she got even a little bit of rest.

When I pulled into my garage, I couldn't believe the curly-haired girl was on my side, coming home with me. I felt like a stranger here after years of living in the same loft. Something about not living here with her didn't feel right.

She clung to my body as I lifted her from the truck. Her hands were around my neck as I cradled her like a baby. I would never stop asking myself what I did to deserve her. Even if the moments I spent with her were limited, it meant the world to me to know that I still meant something to somebody. It meant the world to know I still meant something to her.

She made me feel loved. I wasn't used to that. I didn't know how to act when she cuddled me in bed or woke me up with kisses. After falling asleep to a girl I hooked up with, I never showed them any affection. They never showed it back. The only thing I ever knew how to do was protect her and please her. But Bo made it easy to love her. I didn't feel like a stranger to the newly found emotion.

The elevator doors opened to our home. Instead of the couch, I brought her to our bed. I tucked her in with the blankets before I left for the bathroom. I looked at myself in the mirror, telling myself not to fuck up. I looked at myself and tried not to hate the person staring back at me.

A cry pushed past my lips. I couldn't stand my reflection. How could I ask Bo to forgive me when I can't even look at myself for longer than ten seconds? How could I tell Bo to love me when I don't even like myself? I was asking for the impossible.

"Kinnick?"

Hearing her voice seemed to heal the broken pieces in my heart. "Yeah?"

"I can't sleep."

I walked down the hall to see her sitting up on our bed, rubbing her eyes with a look of exhaustion on her face. "What do you want me to do?"

"Lay with me."

My heartbeat accelerated. "Are you sure you want me to lay with you?"

"I wouldn't want you to lay anywhere else," she murmured.

My feet slowly carried me toward where she lay. I proceeded with caution as my hands peeled back the black comforter. When I slid in next to her body, she put space between us. I worried that this wasn't a good idea. As badly as I wanted to wrap her in my arms and bring her to my chest, I knew I couldn't. This could be my last chance, and I couldn't fuck it up.

Before I could speak to her, slight snores came from her side of the bed. My cheek pressed against the pillow as I turned to see her sleeping. Her eyes rested gently as she perched her cheek on the back of her hands. I felt the corner of my lips tugging upward as I stared at m curly-haired girl in all of her beauty. Maybe I'll be able to rest too.

As my eyes started to flutter shut, I heard a soft mumble. "Don't leave me."

Chapter 16

The palms of my hands hit the cool black sheets, waking me up from my sleep as I dropped my arm in a spot where the curly-haired girl should have been. When my body sat up from the mattress, my eyes were staring at the place Bo used to be. Her bags were missing from the chair, along with the shoes she wore. My head dropped into my hands as I sucked in a heavy breath. Whatever I did, I fucked up, and I don't even know how.

For once, I listened to myself. I thought everything would be different, and I pursued that idea. Whatever was whispering in my ear, I misinterpreted the voice, or maybe I misunderstood what Bo said. Either way, I ended up alone again, and the other half of me was doing god knows what. She walked around the city as if she didn't have my heart in her hands. I was a fucking puppet, and I would do whatever she wanted me to. She could play me as long as it was a guarantee that I still meant something to her, even if it was just a pawn in her game of chess.

My hand reached for the phone on my bedside table, but before I could answer John, a piece of paper fell from my nightstand.

Confusion crashed over my body in waves as I picked up the note on the ground. When I saw Bo's name, I felt a wave of relief drowning me.

"Call me when you wake up."

Without second-guessing, I declined John's call to dial Bo's number. "Hello?"

"Good morning."

"Hi," she spoke softly. "Thank you for calling; I had last-minute paperwork to finish this morning. I didn't want you to assume I left for no reason."

"I wouldn't be upset if you did."

"Well," her voice trailed off. "I wanted to know if you would go out with us tonight."

"Us?"

"Chrissy, Miles, Luke -"

"I don't think that is a good idea," I cleared my throat. "But if you find yourself in the area, you could stop by my place."

There was a slight pause before her voice came through. "It was already on the list."

The corner of my lips tugged upward as my head dropped. "I'll see you later tonight, yeah?"

"Yeah," she murmured. "See you then."

I nodded as if she could see me. "Bye."

Her voice squeaked as it came through. "Bye."

Most days, I found it difficult to get out of bed. There wasn't a reason to open my eyes or slip from the comfort of my sheets. Before her, everything felt normal. I was used to the feeling of my life not going anywhere as if I was on a treadmill, and no matter how much I walked, I stayed in the same spot. After her, I lost the taste of life and how it felt to be loved, and now I want it back.

Now, I have something to look forward to - her. I felt the excitement in my stomach as I waited for the moment we met again. So, as I let the water run over my body in the shower, I thought about the future possibilities.

Could there be an us again, and what would that look like if it happened? What if she didn't love me the same? What would I do if we got back together and she realized she didn't love me like she thought she did? I tried not to think about it, but when it came to Bo, I couldn't shake the negative thoughts.

For the rest of my day, I couldn't figure out how to spend my time. I sat at my kitchen table, trying to figure out how to stop staring at the clock. Every few seconds I spent on the couch, I clicked the lock button on my phone to see the time. So, I sifted through the clothes in my closet, trying to find an outfit.

After changing through most of my clothes, I hurried toward my truck parked in the lot. The hours between me and Bo made me anxious, but I didn't want to miss the moment she walked through my bar's door. So, I beat her to it.

As I pulled behind the building, I wasn't oblivious to the line growing outside. On my way toward the entrance, I stopped by the bouncers. They didn't know what the curly-haired girl was wearing, but they saw the picture on my phone. If she showed up, she doesn't wait in line. Bo comes before everyone else.

I patted Mark's shoulder as I stepped through the doors, and my eyes fell on John immediately. Trevor looked up from the drink he served my trainer, giving me a small wave as he laughed at whatever the green-eyed man in front of him said.

John turned on the barstool, cocking a brow as his eyes searched every inch of my body. "Why are you wearing Gucci loafers?"

My eyes rolled as I looked down at the watch on my wrist. "Why does it matter?"

"You are wearing gray dress pants and satin," he narrowed his eyes at me. "Why are you so dressed up?"

I sighed deeply as Trevor slid me over a ice water. "John, when am I not dressed up?"

"Uh - every day since Bo has left you."

My face fell as I turned to look at him. "How fucking funny."

"Holy shit," Trevor sucked in a deep breath.

As my head peered over my shoulder to follow his gaze, my confusion began to clear up. My lips parted as I stared at the woman dripping in white sequins. Her short, very revealing dress, with a v-line of cleavage, falling below her chest left nothing to question with a slit on her thigh, showing off her hip bone. Three thin diamond straps kept the material together, saving her dress from showing anything else.

Her curls were back in a bun on the top of her head, but I always loved the way she allowed them to fall from the scrunchie to frame her face. Something about Bo seemed dangerously beautiful, and I have always had a thing for danger.

My eyes followed her as she walked toward the bar. The end of her dress hiked up her thigh as she climbed onto a barstool, oblivious to me as I sat three seats away. Trevor reached for a glass underneath the bar before sliding it toward her. A bright smile pulled across her lips as she stared at him with adoration.

For only a second, my eyes steered toward the man coming toward her. Without hesitating, I hurried from my seat. Before he could approach her, I placed my hand on his chest. His drunken eyes looked down at my hand as he raised his arms.

"I don't want any trouble -"

"Then fuck off," I snapped.

Without saying another word, he looked down at Bo and walked away. My body turned to see Bo leaning against the bar with her lip between her teeth as she stared at me. Her leg rested over the other as her arms spread out behind her across the wooden bartop.

"How charming," she slurred.

I pulled at my sleeves as I adjusted the buttons. "That is why they call me Prince Charming."

"No one has every called you that," she snickered.

"You were halfway there," I shrugged, making the curly-haired girl chuckle. "You seem a little drunk, Boston."

"Well, I am walking in heels," she motioned to the rhinestone pumps on her feet. "So, I must not be doing too bad."

"So, you have barely drank anything?"

The corner of her lips tugged upward. "I did at least seven shots."

"Not such an innocent bookworm anymore, huh?"

Her caramel-eyes diverted to her glass as she grabbed it from the bar. "I don't read much anymore."

"Why?" My face scrunched up.

She slowly sipped on her drink before her eyebrows raised. "Luke sold them."

"What?" I choked on disbelief.

"It is fine," her features were etched with sadness. "I'll be fine."

"What made him think that was okay?"

"He said we wouldn't have room for them in the apartment -"

I raked my hand through my hair as I sighed. "Bo -"

"Can we go somewhere that isn't so loud?"

"We can go to my office?" I offered as I nodded toward the hallway.

Without second-guessing, her hand slipped into mine and she dropped off of the stool. I never questioned where Bo led me, even if I knew where we were going. I knew I would follow Bo anywhere the moment she led me into the happiest moments of my life. Somehow, she always knew where to go. So, I never hesitated to follow, and I never will.

Chapter 17

Her fingers curled around my wrist, dragging me down the hallway, away from all of the noise. Before I had a chance to ask if anything was wrong, her palms were slamming me against the wall. I stared down at the curly-haired girl with wide eyes as she cupped the sides of my face and slammed our lips together.

I wanted nothing more than to feel her lips on mine and her body below me as I showed her all of the ways I could take care of her body, but I couldn't do that when she was heavily intoxicated. I pushed her away and watched as her bottom lip pushed out. Small whimpers left her mouth as we broke contact.

My fingers raked through my hair as she leaned against my desk, begging me to kiss her. I watched the tips of her fingers dance along her thighs as she pulled up the sides of her dress. My jaw clenched as she showed me everything she hid underneath her very revealing dress. Her light brown skin glowed under my golden chandelier.

"Please," she begged.

Dirty words left her mouth as she came toward me, running her fingers down my chest. Her small hands undid the buttons of my suit, ripping it open to reveal my skin. My head fell against the wall behind me as her lips planted kisses on my body. I blew out deep breaths as her tongue dragged down my stomach until she was at my belt buckle.

She whispered against my skin. "You know you want this just as much as I do."

"You're drunk," I sighed as she unfasted my belt.

"Then sober me up."

"Not going to happen."

"I didn't drink that much," she pulled away as she jumped into the air with her hand in the sky. "My tolerance is up here."

A chuckle left my lips as I watched the woman I love demonstrate her level of intoxication. "Oh, yeah?"

"Kinnick," she pouted, leaning against me with her head tilted back so I could see her eyes. "I had a bad day, and I need you to help me forget about it."

"Baby," I strained myself from grabbing her face and kissing her. "I am not taking advantage of you when you are drunk. You are going to hate me when you realize what happened."

"I never hated you," she mumbled.

"You are going to if I let this happen."

"Don't you love me?" She stuck her bottom lip out as the corner of her lips tugged upward. "I thought you said you would do anything I asked."

"Bo," I snapped, tearing my eyes away from her body as I rubbed my hand over my face. "I do love you, but I can't -"

"Promise you love me?"

"I promise."

"Then fuck me," her voice dropped dangerously low. "Because I missed you, and I want to remember the feeling of your hands on my body."

I shoved away from the wall, making her gasp as I dropped my hands down to cup her ass. Her legs wrapped around my waist as I lifted her from the ground. She stared down at me as I held her up with amusement in her eyes before she grabbed my face and brought my lips to hers.

I walked her back toward my desk, making sure I fanned my hand over her back to lay her down gently. She watched my every move as if she were waiting for the next, but as her hands pulled down my pants, I pushed her dress up.

"You aren't wearing anything under this?"

She pushed herself onto her elbows. "What was I supposed to wear?"

"Jesus Christ," I rubbed my face. "What am I going to do with you?"

"Whatever you want," the corner of her lips tugged upward.

As my teeth clashed, my jaw clenched at her suggestive tone. My fingertips danced on her thighs, rubbing at the smooth skin as she twitched below me. I watched her wither around as she tried to get my hands closer to the place she ached most for me. My hands curled around her thighs as I yanked her closer to me. Her eyes widened with lust as she gripped the edge of my desk.

Just as her lips parted, begging me to touch her, my fingers pressed into her warm skin. She whimpered as my fingertips gently rubbed in slow circular motions with just enough pressure to make her cry out. As her back arched, I eased my fingers inside of her. She cried as I curled inside of her, bringing pleasure to the features on her face.

"I missed you," I kissed her collarbones.

Her fingers raked through my hair. "Kinnick."

A groan left my mouth as she whispered my name. "Fuck me; I missed you saying my name. It sounds so pretty coming from your mouth."

As her legs began to shake, I watched as she moaned into the silence of my office. Just as her high came to an end, she watched as I placed my tip at her entrance. Her breath hitched as I rocked inside of her, but her eyes never left mine. Her nails gripped my shoulders as I rolled my hips against hers.

She cried into my ear as I gripped her thighs, so she didn't move far away from me as I pushed against her. Fuck me; I've missed this. The feeling of her mouth at my ear as she whines my name and how she begged me not to stop.

"You feel so good," I grumbled in her ear. "Always so fucking ready for me."

The music pounding through the building drowned out her moans as my desk splintered underneath her. Grunts left my lips as her nails found the skin of my shoulders. I knew there would be marks, she left them every time, and I didn't give a fuck. I was hers, and I wanted her to mark me as such.

As I picked up my pace, she couldn't stay quiet. I worried my desk would collapse at any second, but Bo didn't seem to care, and I wouldn't let her fall. She wrapped her arms around my neck as I lifted her from the desk to push her back against the wall. As she sunk onto me, her body shivered.

"Kinnick," she bit my shoulder. "Please -"

"What do you want, baby?"

Our heads were in the clouds, and we were losing our breaths as we reached new heights, growing closer to our peak. She held me tighter to her as I helped her move up and down. Her legs quivered. I kissed the side of her neck as she cried into my shoulder. My name left her lips so much that I could feel my heart clenching.

"I love you, Bo," I squeezed my eyes shut as she clenched against me. "And I miss you. So. Damn. Much."

As I came down from my high, I sat her down on the desk. She whimpered as I pulled out of her. My hands clenched the wood as I found more reasons to repeat what just happened than I did reasons not to, but I couldn't ruin things with the curly-haired girl so I stepped away without another word.

If this was any other time, Bo would have painted her cheeks with a nice shade of embarrassment. Yet, the woman in front of me wasn't phased by what happened. Instead of saying another word, she stepped away from my desk.

"Are you okay?" I mumbled.

Her head slowly moved up and down. "Of course."

"Promise?"

Her smile grew as she stared up at me. "I promise."

"Maybe you should go out first," I nodded toward the door. "We wouldn't want your boyfriend to suspect that anything happened."

Her caramel eyes rolled. "He isn't my boyfriend, Kinnick."

I stepped forward, pressing a soft kiss to her forehead as she moved toward the door. "I'll see you out there."

"See you soon," her playful voice floated through my ears. "Don't make me wait long."

So, I promised I wouldn't before she closed the door behind her. Without wasting time, I hurried to clean myself up. My feet carried me down the hallway as I searched for the curly-haired girl I was alone with only a few short moments ago.

Just as I came around the bar, I caught sight of her chestnut brown coils. My lips morphed into a smile until I saw her more clearly. Slowly, the happiness fell from my face as I stared. Her arms were around Luke's neck as his lips devoured hers. I would have considered it a mistake, but the way she stood on her tippy-toes to press deeper into his kiss made me think otherwise.

My hand snatched a bottle of tequila from the bar. Before I turned around, she looked up to see me. I drowned myself in alcohol as I turned back down the hallway to leave. I could hear her yelling my name as I walked into my office where we just spent an intimate moment together.

"Kinnick -"

My head moved back and forth as I turned to look at her. "You said you weren't together -"

She furrowed her eyebrows. "We aren't -"

"Then what the fuck was that?"

"I am drunk -"

"Drunk?" I choked on laughter. "You used me to get what you wanted."

"I didn't use you."

"If he was enough for you, you wouldn't have begged me to fuck you."

"What am I supposed to do?"

"Not fuck me and then kiss him!"

"Why does it matter? There is nothing going on between you and me!"

And just like that, whatever remained of my heart shattered. "Get out."

"What?"

"Get the fuck out!" My voice raised as I felt the lump in my throat growing.

I never wanted to be the cause of fear in Bo's eyes, but she hurried out of the door as tears fell from her eyes. My hands raked through my hair as I tried to calm the feeling growing in my chest, but a scream of frustration let my lips as I let my fist collide with the wall.

My body fell against the ground as my back slid down the wall. She wasn't mine anymore, and I thought I had time to win her back. I thought we were making progress after she slept at my place and asked me to lay next to her. I thought she wanted me.

I thought she fucking loved me.

Chapter 18

K innick's screams of frustration followed me into the hallway, where I cried. I could hear his fist collide with the wall as the door slammed behind me. I wanted to tell him the kiss meant nothing. After what happened in his office, I wanted to know if Luke could make me feel the way Kinnick did. No matter how hard I pressed my lips against his, it never worked. My heart only belonged to one person, and that one person wanted me to get away.

My feet carried me down the hallway, even though they faltered on the way. I struggled to stand on my own as I walked back toward the bar. A squeak broke through my lips as my body ran into a tattooed boy's chest. I looked up to see Miles staring at me with confusion. I wasn't sure if he heard Kinnick, but the pounding music made it difficult to hear anything.

He wanted to ask if something was wrong, but instead of waiting for him to say something. I knew he was calling my name, but I didn't care as I stepped away. My eyes met John's face of remorse as he came toward me. It made me wonder if everyone knew what happened.

"Is everything okay?"

"What makes you think it isn't?"

He nodded toward the hallway, asking me to follow him. I trailed behind John as he led me down the corridor to a separate room. He fell back onto the couch as he looked at me with worry. It was as if he had a million questions, but his face made him appear scared to ask.

"I heard Kinnick," he trailed off.

My face fell into my hands. "He saw me kissing Luke."

"Oh -"

"I didn't kiss him because I have feelings for him," I cried out. "I wanted to see if he could make me feel how Kinnick did."

"Why?"

My voice cracked. "It would be easier to walk away."

"You can't walk away when it is real."

Tipsy John spoke straight to my soul, and it wasn't long into our conversation that he was convincing me to sneak out of the back door. Our bodies stumbled down the streets of our city as we moved slowly toward the McDonald's down the road. He promised it would cure my broken heart. So, we stood in the lobby, ordering whatever seemed pleasing off of the menu. Instead of staying in the lobby, the employees asked us to leave.

Now I am sitting in front of my best friend, eating french fries smothered in ranch as we hum to different tunes in our heads. It made me realize how much I missed John but how different our relationship was now that we had overcome the past. I felt closer to him than ever.

"Luke thinks we are together," I said as if he wanted to hear me rant about boys. "What is he going to do when I tell him that I slept with Kinnick?"

"Who cares as long as you are happy?"

My shoulders shrugged as I sucked down the sprite in my cup. Just as I opened my mouth to bite into the chicken nugget in my hand, I looked up to see Trevor walking through the door. He furrowed his eyebrows as he stared in amusement. His eyebrow arched as he stared down at the McDonald's between John and me. His tattooed hand reached out, snatching a french fry from my box.

"Hey!"

He winked down at me. "What are you weirdos doing anyway?"

"Eating," I rolled my eyes. "What does it look like, T?"

He smiled at my nickname. "It looks like you guys are up to no good."

"Trouble is our middle name," I shrugged, spinning in the office chair.

"Your boyfriend is looking for you," his head moved back and forth as he laughed.

"Which one?" John snickered, making me gasp.

I threw a french fry at him as I stood up. "Asshole."

John's laughter filled the room as he stood up to hug me. "If you need somewhere to stay, call me."

Luke waited at the bar, watching as Trevor leaned down to kiss my cheek before leaving me alone with the man I used to call my best friend. The second no one was around; Luke started asking questions. He wanted to know why I kissed him and if it meant anything to me as it did to him, but I knew I couldn't say a thing as he asked with a dark tone to his voice. I followed him toward the car where Miles waited.

"Are you okay, best friend?"

"Always."

"You know I am always here for you, right?"

I grinned up at him as he opened my door. "My prince."

"Anything for my princess."

When we made it to the apartment, I felt the alcohol settling in my stomach. The nauseous feeling begged me to lay down. So, I carried myself to my room, where Luke didn't trail too far behind. His heavy footsteps made my emotions stir with anxiety as he followed me into my bedroom.

"Where were you all night?"

"I went with John to McDonald's."

His hands motioned to me. "Wearing that?"

"I was with John."

"Bo, I don't even know who he is," he threw his hands in the air. "How do I know he can keep you safe?"

"Did you even realize I was gone?"

"I saw you disappear with Kinnick."

"And? Nothing is going on between you and I."

"What happened between you two?"

"None of that is any of your business."

"You can't keep leading me on -"

"I made it clear that I was using you to forget, Luke."

"So, what? You are back with him now?"

"No -"

"But you slept with him, didn't you?" His voice hardened. "That is where you were all night."

"It doesn't matter!" I snapped. "I don't love you, Luke. You are not him, and you never will be. Do you understand that? My heart will always belong to Kinnick."

"Are you fucking kidding me? After everything he did -"

My back turned to him as I felt the exhaustion sweeping over me. "Luke, go to bed."

"Don't turn your back on me."

I didn't worry about his threat until I collided with the wall. My face smacked the surface as he pushed against me. I whimpered the moment he flipped me around to look at him. My nose throbbed as I felt liquid pouring over my mouth. My shaky hands reached up, touching my lips to see my fingertips covered in blood.

He stared at the blood dripping down my face as he pinned me to the wall. Just as his lips parted to speak, the bedroom door flew open. I watched fingers curl over Luke's shoulder before he was yanked backward. Miles hurried toward me to inspect my injury, but I held up my hands to stop him as I moved toward the purse on my nightstand. My hand snatched the bag with my keys before I hurried toward my bedroom door.

I kicked off my heels at the door before hurrying down the hallway. Sobs left my lips as my nose throbbed in pain. I couldn't see through my blurry vision. Miles called out to me as I stumbled down the stairs, but I made it out the door before he could catch me.

My shaky hand gripped the steering wheel as I turned over the car. I didn't know where to go. I wanted to go to Kinnick, but he didn't want me, even if what he assumed was wrong. My fingers stumbled over the screen of my phone as I searched for his number.

"Bo?"

I wiped the blood from my nose as his voice came from the other side of my phone. "Is the door to the elevator unlocked?"

"Always."

"I am on my way -"

"Bo," he sighed.

"Please," I choked on a sob.

"What happened? His tone changed. "Where are you?"

Before I ended the call, I answered. "I am almost there."

Chapter 19

When Miles called late in the night, I wasn't sure how to answer. Things felt different after I put my hands on Chrissy and hit him. But the second my thumb slid across my screen; his frantic voice came through. Everything that happened between us didn't matter because my mind trailed off to the safety of Bo.

My fingers drifted through my hair as he explained what happened moments prior to calling. He barged into their bedroom after hearing a commotion, and he found Luke pinning my curly-haired girl to the wall with blood pouring from her nose.

As he voiced his concern about her driving under the influence, the chains in the elevator began to rattle. The numbers on the panel above the doors started to change, and I knew that she would be coming up any second.

I stood in front of the doors, telling Miles that everything would be okay. The moment the bell started to ding, I waited for her the metal to separate. My finger ended the call as my curly-haired girl walked into my dimly lit apartment with crimson stains on her dress.

The skin I caressed earlier and the lips I kissed prior to now were covered with dried blood. My jaw clenched as I narrowed my eyes at the girl on the verge of a panic attack. Her bare feet hit the ground running as she shot for me with her arms wide open. I covered her with protection as my arms ran down her bareback.

Her tears wet my shirt as she cried into my chest. I clenched my fists as I pulled her deeper into my safety. After pulling her into the bathroom to gently wipe the blood from her nose, I brought her to our bed to rest. Now she is sleeping, and I am in the gym, letting my fists collide with the bag as I think of Luke.

The scars on my knuckles split open soon after the first collision, staining the bag. John would be pissed, but I needed to feel something other than the ache in my veins telling me to find the piece of shit who put his hands on my girl. I thought laying next to Bo would soothe me, but the more I stared down at the bruise forming on her face, the more I found myself unable to sit still.

As the seven o'clock sun rose over the horizon, it touched the gym with a warm glow. My eyes struggled to focus as the light glared off of the mirror. The heat made me uncomfortable as hitting a bag didn't fix how I felt. Not even after hours of hitting it. Nothing would heal the anger in my veins until my fingers were wrapped around his throat, draining the air from his lungs.

The music playing through my headphones cut off as John's name flashed across my screen. "What?"

He cleared his throat, and his words came out shaky. "Hey, do you know where Bo is?"

My eyebrows furrowed as I put the phone to my ear. "Why are you talking like that?"

"Well, Luke has a reason to believe she is with you."

"Where are you?"

"The bar," John spoke. "He is threatening Trevor."

"Perfect," I cracked my neck. "I'm down the street."

I knew getting behind the wheel would be a mistake. My hands were shaking, and I knew it would be impossible to control the wheel as I drove down the street. That didn't stop me from reaching for the gun in my glove compartment and tucking it into the band of my shorts. Revenge was flooding my veins, and I wasn't sure what was going to happen.

As I reached the front door of the bar, I gripped the front door without hesitation and ripped it open. The moment I stepped through, I saw him in Trevor's face. Before he could say another word, I shoved him into the counter. When he collided with the wood, a gasp left his mouth. He turned around with anger in his eyes, but he didn't say a word.

"You want to talk shit when I am not here," I shrugged. "Where is that energy now?"

"Where is Bo?"

The second her name came out of his mouth; my fist crossed his face. He spat blood onto the ground as he fell to the ground. John yelled out at me as I pulled my foot back long enough to gain the momentum to drive it into Luke's stomach. A cry of pain left the lips of the boy on the floor.

My knees burned as they skid across the floor long enough to climb on Luke. I wasn't sure if my knuckles were still bleeding from earlier or if it was Luke's blood all over his face, but I wasn't satisfied if it was his. I felt the stinging sensation ripping through my hand as my knuckles busted open the bridge of his nose. When his head snapped back, John screamed behind me to stop.

"Kinnick, you are going to kill him!"

I shoved him away, unable to care as he fell to the floor. My fingers gripped the collar of Luke's hoodie as I placed him on his feet. As I stood face to face with him, I could feel the fire spreading further through my body. He struggled to stand up as I released him.

"You can't do it, though. Can you?" His voice floated through the bar.

"What?" I cocked a brow as I turned back toward him.

"You always talk about killing someone, but where is that energy when it comes down to it?"

My shoulders shrugged as I pulled the gun from my waistband. John's nails were short, but they broke my skin open as he attempted to pull me backward. Luke's eyes flashed as I rushed toward him. My body shoved his into the wall; my forearm pressed into his throat as I brought the metal to his temple. When my finger pulled the trigger and let it click, his eyes widened.

"You fucking psychopath!" When my hands released him, I watched his demeanor change. "You could have killed me."

"Without hesitating."

"You knew there were no bullets in there -"

My fingers released the cylinder latch, watching as the revolver's cylinder swung from the frame. I pressed into the ejector rod, letting the bullets fall to the ground below us. As the metal collided with the ground, his lips parted.

"When it happens, and it will happen, I will stare into your eyes as my bullets drain every ounce of blood from your body," the corners of my lips twitched. "And when I fall asleep next to my girl, I'll be able to rest knowing there is one last piece of shit in the world that could hurt her."

He looked between me and the casings on the floor before moving toward the entrance doors. As I tossed the gun onto the table, I rubbed my face with bloodied hands. What the fuck was I going to tell Bo?

I looked up at John and Trevor, who was staring at me with wide eyes. "Don't look at me like."

"Do you just wake up and choose violence?" John blinked a few times at a rapid pace.

"Violence chooses me."

"That isn't funny."

A smile pulled across my lips. "You act like I was going to kill him."

"You could have -"

"Could have," I reminded him.

"Your ability to act normally after that proves that you are indeed a psychopath," Trevor chimed in.

If the shoes fit, I'll wear it. My shoulders tipped upward as I walked out of the bar without so much as another word. There is a difference between beating the shit out of someone because they deserved it and just beating the shit out of somebody. I would like to think I was in the gray area. When I made it home, I wanted to give Bo something that would distract her from everything that happened.

As I pulled around to the window of the Scooter's drive-thru, I pulled money from my wallet. Ready to pay, I reached out the window to hand the barista the twenty in between my fingers. The moment the window opened, a gasp left her lips, and my order fell from her hands. I jumped as the cool substance of Bo's smoothie collided with my face.

"I am so sorry - there is blood -"

"Oh, I know."

"Uh - I -"

"Just remake my order and take the money."

As my fingers drummed on the steering wheel, I realized how badly this all looked. Dried blood cracked on my fingers, flaking and breaking off. I raised my eyes to the rearview mirror and sighed. What the fuck was I going to tell Bo? Splatters of crimson covered my face.

"Sir," a shaky voice talked beside me.

I turned to see the small barista and gave her a crooked grin. "Thanks."

She opened her mouth but quickly shut it as she handed me the bag of blueberry muffins and a drink holder filled with smoothies. On the ride home, I looked at the drinks beside me and knew this wouldn't be enough. As I pulled into the parking lot, I hoped the curly-haired girl would be sleeping still. It would allow me time to clean up and throw out the clothes.

When the elevator doors separated, the apartment sat still. Not a sound came from the bedroom. I gently stepped around the wooden floors, hoping to keep silent as I made it to the bathroom door. My clothes fell into a pile on the floor as I slipped behind the shower door. Steam filled the small space, soothing the aches in my muscles.

"Kinnick?"

A series of curse words fell from my lips as I heard her feet padding on the floor. "Give me a minute. I'll be out."

I heard the bathroom door creak open as she came inside. "My face hurts."

The cracking of her voice made me want another chance to hit Luke. "I'm coming."

Before I could shut off the water, I heard the door behind me open. "Bo -"

A gasp left her lips as she looked at the sea of blood below her. "Are you okay?"

"I got into a fight."

"When? It is eight in the morning. You are aware of that, right?"

"I couldn't sleep, so I went to the gym. John called me and told me Luke was at the bar causing Trevor trouble."

"You beat up Luke?"

"Yes," I waited for her to get upset. "He deserved it."

"I am waiting for the rest of the story."

"What are you talking about?"

"The gun next to the blueberry muffins."

I choked out a laugh. "I'm not good at hiding shit."

"No," a smile spread across her lips. "You aren't."

My fingers ran along her hips as I pulled her into my chest. "All you need to know is he is not going to be a problem anymore."

She slapped her hand over her mouth. "You killed him?"

"Do you think I would actually do that?"

She broke eye contact as she nodded. "Yeah, kind of."

"Why would you stay around if you thought I killed somebody?"

"Well, I just found out," she teased. "I haven't had time to run yet."

"Funny," I grumbled.

Her thumbs brushed over my face. "I trust you."

Her movements were gentle as she scrubbed over the dried blood. I watched as she frowned at the broken skin on my knuckles. The longer she inspected made me furrow my brows. It was as if she was waiting for my bone to pop out. My eyes looked over the face of the woman I loved more than anyone in the world, wondering how I got her back here with me. After last night, I thought I would never have this chance again.

I caressed the side of her face as I cupped her chin with my fingers. "Are you scared of me?"

"Why would I be scared of you?"

"You are washing blood off my body."

"Honestly?" She pressed deeper into my hold as I ran my hand along the side of her cheek. "The only thing I feared was wondering when we would run out of time together."

"What are you talking about?"

Her eyes fluttered open as she stared up at me. "I don't want until death do us part because I never wish to be parted from you from this day on. And perhaps that is what I fear more than anything - when this is all over, and our days have finally come to their end, what if you aren't waiting for me on the other side?"

My eyes met her caramelized ones that were full of sadness and swirling with despair. "When you left, everything went dark. But whenever my hands would reach for something intended to do me harm, a little voice told me to put it down. If I was going down the wrong path, that voice told me to steer in a different direction. When I thought I couldn't take it anymore, it told me to hang on, so I did."

"Kinnick -"

"The same night being away from you became too much, I left my apartment like that little voice asked, and I walked around the city for hours without a destination until I found you then I realized the purpose of my journey," my voice cracked. "Things are too much of a coincidence to not be real. When you are around, my heart beats a little faster as if it is signaling to me that you are my person -"

"So, if I am not waiting for you on the other side when all of this is over, it is because I am on my way," my fingertips ran along her skin. "Just promise that even when your feet hurt, exhaustion is sweeping over your body, and that little voice inside of your head is telling you to leave, you will wait for me."

Her fingers laced with mine as she gently began to squeeze. "As long as you promise me the same."

I pressed my forehead against hers as my eyes fluttered shut. "My whole life has been a series of waiting for you, Boston Bennett. I wouldn't have spent it doing anything else."

Chapter 20

Everyone wanted to know my opinion on true happiness as if I had the answer. People asked if it was the feeling I got after knocking out an opponent just to experience a belt getting wrapped around my waist. The assumption was that I would never have to worry about the rest of my life because my funds would support me, even after death. Happiness didn't come from stepping onto the street where everyone knew my name, but after years of trying to decipher it, I figured out what it meant to me.

As my back pressed into the wooden chair, I stared at the woman before me as she ate blueberry muffins and sipped on a fresh pot of warm coffee. Her puffy morning skin glowed in the soft morning sun. Her eyes fluttered softly as she struggled to stay awake while her teeth broke down the food in her mouth. I brought the yellow coffee mug to my lips and stared at the woman before me.

Happiness was sharing blueberry muffins and coffee with Bo. Well, happiness was anything that involved the curly-haired girl. It was the way her fingers curled around the handle of her cup and how she softly chewed as if she were trying to savor both. The pace of my breathing quickened at the sight of her yawning. Somehow everything she did knocked me the fuck out -

"Why are you staring at me?" She swallowed harshly before gently setting down her muffin.

"Because it's you," my palm rubbed over my face. "And everything about you."

"What is that supposed to mean?"

"How dare you hold my heart the way you do?" My teeth ground against one another. "You have it on such a tight fucking leash, and it hasn't tried to run once. It has been totally devoted to you, but you have not let up on your grip. I never asked for distance to part us, and yet, you continue to experiment on my heart as if you are some fucking scientist -"

"You - you," I stumbled over my words as I stood from my seat. "You sit here, eating your breakfast so softly that it makes my heart pound. You sit here with a look on your face that says you are thinking about something, and I am over here, wondering what I have to fucking do to listen to all of it. Nothing in my life has made me pray, but I have talked about you so many times to God that he doesn't have time to listen to anything else -"

"I constantly beg him to restore my eyesight so that I can see you clearly," I choked. "For half of my life, I have struggled to see. When I didn't have anything to look forward to, I stopped searching. But Boston, in every crowded room, through the spotting blocking my eyesight, I will always look for you. And you have the audacity to ask why I am staring at you -"

"I am trying to memorize your face," I couldn't sit still as I grew uncomfortable. "From the shape of your hairline to the dimples in your cheek. Your curl type and every way you wear it. How your caramel eyes look for me the second your eyes open from sleeping all night. I want to remember how your skin glows and how you look at me when you say how much you love me -"

"You are it for me, Boston Bennett," I gasped for air. "And I want you now, in the next five minutes, an hour from this moment to forever. It will only ever be you and how you choose to love me despite all of the horrible fucking things I have done."

"What am I supposed to say to you?" Her lips parted as tears welled in her eyes. "How am I supposed to respond to that, Kinnick? I -"

"I want to know that you love me still," I motioned to myself. "I want to know that you want me as badly as I want you!"

"I will always want you!" Her voice raised. "Is that not clear? I am here, aren't I? I slept in your bed, didn't I? We just showered together, did we not?"

"That isn't enough," my heart pounded. "I want you to tell me that you'll never leave me as you once did. Tell me you love me."

"I do love you," her hands collided with the table. "I have only ever loved you!"

"I want you to not question my intentions," I pleaded. "I want you to know that I speak with honesty and promise every time I say how much I love you."

"But you hurt me," she whimpered.

"Not intentionally," I walked toward her. "I would never cause you harm, Bo. Please, tell me you know I would never do anything to hurt you."

"What if I break your heart?"

The corner of my lips tugged upward as I shook my head in disbelief. "Oh, break it, Bo. Don't stop there, though. Rip it out, tear it apart, fucking step on it; I don't care. Do whatever you want to me so that I can feel the things that only you make me feel. Do it for the rest of your life, and don't ever fucking stop."

"I don't do it on purpose -"

"No, but I want you to," I pleaded. "You are the only person close enough to my heart that is truly capable of ripping me apart. Please, make me feel like I will never recover because I want the pain; I want the tears and the happiness. Give me all of it. I want every fucking piece of you that you are willing to offer."

She placed her palms against my chest as I cupped her cheek gently. "Oh, do what you want with me, Boston Bennett. Do it all."

"Then do one thing for me," she murmured as her eyes stared into mine.

"Anything," my breath fanned across her lips as I felt her warmth against me.

"Kiss me," her strained words lost air. "Kiss me and promise that you will do it until both of us are gasping for a breath and you think my lips are the very thing that will give you air."

Before I connected our lips, she spoke one last time. "But one last thing, please?"

"What is it?" My fingertips brushed away her hair as I ached to feel her lips against mine.

"Love me how you do and only how you can do," my forehead rested against hers. "And don't ever change yourself thinking I would want you any other way."

"I promise," I kissed the tip of her nose. "I promise it all."

Her mouth brushed against mine. "Then I don't know why you are taking so long to kiss me."

Chapter 21

The way her lips molded against mine made it easy to relax. These past few years, I stood on the edge. The curly-haired girl's hand is in mine, bringing me back from the ledge as I dared to jump. Now my body is falling back onto the bed of my satin sheets as she climbed on top of me. It was how she whispered how much she missed me on my lips that coaxed me back from the doors of insanity, but I knew what I felt for her wasn't sane.

My hands were hesitant to touch her body as if police marked her skin with caution tape. Never have I been the one to follow the rules, but if she had built a wall of boundaries, I wouldn't be the one to knock them down. I couldn't be the wrecking ball this time. So, I would stand at the doors until she opened them again.

Just as she started tugging at the bottom of my shirt, the sound of distant ringing broke us apart. I pressed myself onto my elbows as she climbed off my lap. Confusion painted my expression as her reddened cheeks were the last thing I saw before she slipped away. Bo had never been nervous with me unless we were doing something she wasn't accustomed to, but we have kissed plenty of times. Yet, I am sitting here, wondering what I did wrong.

When her voice started floating through the apartment, I stood from my bed to discover if something had happened. My fingers raked through my hair as I walked through the hallway before finding her in the living room. She paced the floor, smiling at whatever the other person said. It wasn't that I wanted to be the only thing that made her happy, but I wanted to qualify. Lately, it doesn't feel like I am good enough to rank.

My shoulder leaned against the doorway as I stared at her with my arms crossed over my body. "Everything okay?"

She tucked her phone away as she nodded. "Yeah - that was John."

"Oh."

"He was calling to make sure everything was okay."

My head bobbed softly as I stepped toward her. "And what did you say?"

"Aside from the pain, everything is perfect."

"You can go lay down; I'll bring you something."

As she walked down the hallway, she stopped near my side long enough to press a kiss on my bare shoulder. My eyes fluttered shut as the gentle touch made my muscles relax. When her phone started to ring, I worried that someone planned on taking her away from me. As the distant sound of her feet padding against the hardwood floors turned silent, I pushed away from the wall to find pain relievers.

The pills rattled in the bottle as I snatched them from the kitchen counter. My feet padded on the ground, carrying me closer to her. Before I could step through the corridor of my bedroom, I saw her reading over a stack of papers on my dresser. My shoulder pressed into the doorway as I watched her read over whatever information I laid at her disposal. My eyebrows furrowed in confusion as she looked up from the documentation with parted lips.

My gaze fell to the ground because the look in her eyes is one I have seen enough in my life to understand that even the woman I love most in this world fears me. I clenched my jaw to hold back the dam of emotions crashing against the walls I had built up not to show any emotion.

"You were the one who fractured that man's jaw."

My eyes gently shut. "Bo -"

"The report said the man's alcohol levels were so high," she choked. "It was past the legal limit."

As guilt flushed through my body, she continued talking. "I saw the pictures. It was a week after I was attacked, and my firm asked me to take the case, but after what happened, I couldn't. His eye socket had been fractured. Plastic surgeons installed metal plates into his jaw to reinforce the bone structure. How could you do that to somebody, Kinnick? What would even push you to that point?"

"I don't know," I mumbled through heavy emotions. "I can't remember -"

"You can't remember?" She choked. "That man is suffering right now, and you can't even remember why you did it -"

"Please," I shake my head. "Just stop."

"Why do you insist on being the man everyone says you are?"

My gaze lifted from the floor. "Because I am that man."

"No, you are not!"

"I hurt people, Bo!" My voice echoed through the apartment. "That is what I fucking do!"

"You aren't that man -"

"Then why did you leave me?" I snapped. "If I don't hurt people, why aren't you at home with me? Why can't you fucking talk to me without your hands shaking? If I didn't hurt people, you would still be here."

"I am standing in front of you, right now!"

"But your fucking mind is elsewhere!" My voice raised. "Do you think I cannot see that shit? I notice everything about you, Bo. When you talk to me, your fingers start to twitch. When I walk into a room, your breath hitches. I don't still you anymore."

"I don't know how to act around you -"

"You don't have to act," I gestured toward her. "Just be your fucking self."

"How?" She let out a scream. "I don't even know who I am anymore!"

"And I still love you," my jaw clenched. "Every version of yourself that you gave me, I loved. Every inch. Every bit. I fucking loved all of you."

"I love you, Kinnick," she sighed. "You'll have me in a way that no one else ever will, but -"

"If you are going to give me a shit reason we can't be together, then fucking leave because I cannot keep doing this."

She swallowed harshly as her eyes glossed over. "Kinnick, there are a million reasons as to why we shouldn't be together, but here I am, standing in front of you, holding onto the one reason that makes me stay."

"I have nothing to fucking offer you," my voice cracked the hard tone, making me realize she was the only person that made me crumble. "I don't need you or anyone else to tell me I don't deserve you; I knew that the night I saw you at the party. But for once, I wondered when it was my fucking turn to win."

"Kinnick -"

"I think you should leave."

"Wait -"

"No," a tear smacked the wooden floor below me before I could brush it away to stare at the girl before me. "It's time to go."

Without saying another word, she moved toward her sandals next to my bed. I watched her small feet slip into her flip-flops as she snatched her keys from the end table. The sound of her keys sounded like warning bells. Something told me she wasn't coming back if I let her walk through that door, but I wasn't going to reach out to stop her.

Just as I heard the elevator ding, I collapsed to my knees. She was fucking leaving me again, and for the first time, I did nothing to stop her. In fact, I would encourage her to get as far away from me as she could.

Chapter 22

- -

The breeze drifted through the pine trees surrounding Trevor's mom's backyard. As my back leaned against the wooden lawn chair, I watched the string of lights sway back and forth above us. Golden rays cast down from the Edison Bulbs, bringing a glow that the bonfire could not. I listened to the wood crackle as it crumbled in the heat. It felt like high school again, partying at Trevor's place when his parents were home.

The cabin-styled home's large windows reminded me of the curly-haired girl. It reminded me of the first time I noticed how quickly I began falling for Bo and how she stepped onto the back patio with my hoodie on. It reminded me of the same night she came to snuggle up on my lap as she promised to stay up all night. Now I am staring at the marshmallow bag, wondering what wouldn't remind me of her? For she was the best at roasting the perfect marshmallow.

Now I am thinking about last week and how I made her leave. I couldn't watch her do it on her own, though. So, I didn't give her an option; I made the curly-haired girl walk without hesitating. As

I lifted myself from the chair, I left my friends to find something I could sip on that wouldn't make me fall into a downhill spiral. Maybe I could find something that helped me forget about her. Trevor didn't drink anymore, so I knew I would find something sitting around somewhere.

My eyes fell on the Hawaiian Punch, realizing it was either that or nothing, so I sucked in a deep breath before pouring a red solo cup full. It tasted like the mix I made Bo when she wanted to play beer pong but told me how much she hated beer. My fingers ran through my hair as I tried to pull her from my thoughts.

"I didn't know you'd be here."

My head rolled to the side to see Chrissy standing beside me, and suddenly I wanted to leave. "Likewise."

"So, Bo has been staying with you, I assume?"

My eyebrows furrowed as I brought the cup away from my lips. "No -"

"Well, she hasn't been home," she stared up at me with confusion. "I assumed she was staying with you -"

"Bo!" Trevor's voice echoed through the backyard. "I am glad you could make it."

I snapped my head to the side to see the caramel-eyed woman walking through the fence with her long curls falling down her back. She stepped toward Trevor in her spandex-looking shorts and crop-top t-shirt. She wrapped her arms around his neck before giving him a soft kiss on the cheek.

My hand gripped the plastic tighter as I heard him ask her if she slept okay. It only made me assume she stayed at his house, and that could be the reason she handed him a small silver key. Before the blonde girl beside me could say a word, the cup crumbled under my hold. The punch splattered over us both, making her gasp out of surprise.

"Kinnick -"

"I don't want to hear it," I snapped.

I tossed the cup into the trashcan beside the table before heading toward the sliding glass doors. My hand rubbed over my face as I tried to rid it of the red liquid. My hand shoved the bathroom door shut as I sat in the bathroom, trying to understand why this shit kept fucking happening to me.

Before I could take a breath, the door handle started to jiggle. My head fell into my hands as I tried to take a deep breath. The knob moved again, making me stand up to yank the door open. Just as I went to snap at the person standing before me, I realized the curly-haired girl was the one in my presence.

"Sorry," she squeaked. "I'll come back -"

"No," I shake my head. "I was just leaving."

Without saying another word, I walked around her. I think I am wrong, but I thought I caught her watching me as I walked down the stairs. Something makes me hope I am not. So, I held onto the idea that she still loves me despite yelling at her last week to leave. Now I am grabbing my jacket from the back of the couch before leaving so I don't keep believing in things that I know aren't true.

"To what do I owe the pleasure?"

My eyes lifted from the couch to see Rosie with a drink in her hand. "I didn't know you were coming."

"Surprise," she grinned. "What are you doing hiding in here by yourself?"

"I am not hiding," I grumbled.

"Mhm," her hand slipped into mine. "Let's get you a drink."

"I don't drink -"

"Not even punch?"

My eyes rolled at her. "The last time you got me punch, it tasted like shit."

"Well, tell John that because he picked it out."

A chuckle pushed past my lips. "So, you telling me what Trevor has is going to taste better."

"Of course," she smiled up at me. "Who do you think picked it out?"

"Oh," I cocked my brows in amusement.

She pressed a cup to my chest. "Orange sherbert. My favorite."

"Is this a party or a kid's birthday?"

"It can't be an actual party because some people don't know how to handle their alcohol," her hip bumped mine as she winked.

"Funny," I snorted.

"You know I love you."

I bent down, kissing the top of her head. "So you say."

"Come on," she laced our hands. "Let's go find a seat."

"Rosie, I didn't plan on staying -"

"Why?"

A familiar burst of laughter filled the night, giving me goose-bumps as it always did when I heard it. I saw the girl with curly hair standing next to Miles with her head tipped back as her happiness fell from her mouth in a beautiful melody. This is why you shouldn't let the person you fall for meet your friends because they will fall for them too, and you cannot spend the rest of your life after your break-up acting like they don't exist.

Rosie stared up at me with her eyes widening in despair, but mine stayed on the girl who owned my heart. It wasn't seeing her that made me feel saddened. No, it was the way that seeing her made me calm. All of the noises in my head ceased to exist as if all of my demons ached to hear her voice and craved for her next move. She silenced my mind and soothed my soul. Bo gave me a feeling no one else ever has, so I struggle to answer if it is real just because I cannot name it.

"We spent all night talking about you," Trevor came into view. "She asked me what you were like growing up. She wanted to know all of the stupid things you did and if you have always been so stubborn. And then she asked me if you ever told another girl you love her, but I couldn't remember a time you ever said it to anybody."

Because I didn't, I never said anything I didn't believe. I couldn't even remember the last time I said it to my mom. I wouldn't speak of love if it didn't exist, but the night I saw the curly-haired girl on that disgusting couch in her sweatpants smiling underneath the shitty living room lighting, I knew I had been wrong all along. Maybe love didn't exist, but she did, and that was pretty fucking close.

Chapter 23

A s I sat in the lawn chair, rubbing my fingers against one another, my leg bouncing out of frustration, I listened to the
curly-haired girl demonstrate to everyone how to roast the perfect
marshmallow. It wasn't that Bo thought she actually perfected a
roasted marshmallow, but everyone else did, and now they are
hanging on her every word as she giggles because the caramel-eyed
girl thinks they are joking.

I am the only one without a stick in his hand. When I wrote out
what I wanted to do today, this wasn't at the top of the list, and quite
honestly, it never would be. I didn't care how to make the perfect
roasted marshmallow.

Yet, Trevor is on the edge of his seat, smiling as if falling in love
for the first time. He finds the girl in front of him infatuating. So, he
is willing to do whatever he has to just so that she notices him, even
if it is for a split second. See if Trevor had a to-do list; at the top of
it would be written, 'whatever I can do to make Bo notice me.'

It isn't like I would hate him if she chose him at this point. As
a matter of fact, I would silently root for them. Maybe he could

make her happy, and I would finally get what I deserved for not only hurting the girl I loved the most in this world but for being the person my best friend's girlfriend cheated on him with.

So, he continues to stare ahead at the curly-haired girl, hoping that she will look up and notice him. Me? I am staring at Bo as if my doctor just told me I am losing my eyesight tomorrow, and I am doing whatever I can to memorize every detail of her face before then.

The difference between Trevor and me? She'll break his heart. Actually, she is going to rip it from his fucking chest. Bo will stomp on it as she stares up at him with a smile on her face, and those little dimples I love so much will show up. But she has already done that to me, and I won't ever be able to feel that again. So, that makes him a lucky fucking man. I would give my life to have that woman bring me the pain so that I can feel her again.

"Are you okay?" Rosie leaned into me.

My eyes blinked a few times until I finally tore them away from Bo. "Yeah."

"Do you want me to get you something?"

I moved my head back and forth. "No, I am heading out for the night."

"Why?"

"I've got court in the morning," I cleared my throat.

"Do you want us to be there?" Miles looked up at me.

Before I could stop it, I snapped. "No, I don't."

Without saying another word, I grabbed my keys from the plastic table and left. I could hear them talking, but I didn't want to focus on their words. When I leave, I don't look at their faces. It is a reminder of what I already know - I am a disappointment to my friends and they know they can never rely on me for anything, so I never ask them for support.

It isn't like I have court tomorrow anyway, though. That isn't until Monday, and I know everyone saw through my shit, but nobody questioned me when I said it. They let me walk away because when I get like this, I know I scare everyone, and I want to disappear because of it.

It wasn't that I didn't want them to be there when my therapist tells the judge if I made any progress. I don't want my friends to be sitting behind me when the judge tells me I am being sentenced again. They watched me get dragged away by the cops before, I won't let them witness that again. I don't want the only memories I have with my friends to be me going to jail because I cannot learn how to stop doing stupid shit.

"Hey."

I looked over my shoulder to see the curly-haired girl behind fiddling with her fingers. "Hey."

"I work for the law firm that has your case," she cleared her throat. "I know you don't have court tomorrow."

I gently shut the driver's side door before leaning against my truck with my arms crossed to look at the girl who stared at me with furrowed eyebrows. "You came all the way out here to tell me that?"

"It isn't like you to lie, Kinnick."

"Why do you care, Boston?"

"Is it a crime that I do?"

"I didn't say that," my head moved back and forth. "I am asking why you care."

"Despite the idea that everything we had was a lie, I still love you."

"That is why you ran to Trevor, right?"

"Actually, Trevor stayed here last night, and I stayed at his apartment," a frown settled into her face. "Rosie was there too just in case you want to brush up on your facts."

"What was Rosie doing at Trevor's apartment?"

"They've been seeing one another," she sighed. "You would know that if you asked, but you didn't. You just assume the worst from your friends."

"You want me to believe he is actually interested in her? He couldn't keep his fucking eyes off of you all night."

"You need to stop before you lose this friendship -"

"Lose it? It's already fucking lost."

"Why? Because you cannot understand that there is nothing happening between me and him -"

"No, Boston because I fucked his girlfriend," I seethed. "And now I am worried the same thing is going to happen to me -"

"Charlie?" She choked out before I could finish.

"Yeah," my head moved back and forth. "How do you know Charlie?"

"How do I know my best friend's cousin?"

My face fell as I stared at her. "Bo -"

"When?"

"Don't make me answer that."

"When did it happen?"

As the curly-haired girl stood in front of me with tears welling in her eyes, I knew I fucked up again. Somehow I always fucked up when it came to this woman. Sometimes I wondered how that could be when I looked myself in the mirror every night and asked myself to not fuck this up. Now I have to look her in the caramel eyes that I love so much and tell her that I fucked her best-friends cousin the same night she found out about the wreck.

"The night you found out -" before I could finish a sob ripped through her throat, and I didn't stop, I just kept going. "We were supposed to go to a party. Everyone kept asking where you were, but I didn't care about anything other than getting my mind off of it all. After taking shots, we ended up in my office -"

"Stop," she cried. "Just stop."

"Bo -"

She waved her hand at me, ceasing all sound from my lips as she silently begged me to stop. As she pressed her palm against her mouth, I listened to muffle her sobs before turning away from me. My body pressed deeper into my truck as I fell back in defeat. The street around me sounded like her crying as she walked back into the yard, and all I could do was watch her.

A heavy breath left my lips. "I'm sorry."

Chapter 24

The woman in front of me talked about my recent decisions, and she analyzed them as if I couldn't decipher when they started to go wrong in the first place. My eyes were focused on the window pane, though. The water trickling down the glass reminded me of the moments I loved the most with Bo. She seemed the most authentic when the skies were gray and rumbling. So, I watched the raindrops fall until my therapist asked if I was listening. Then I would turn my head back toward her and nod to the words she spoke until I convinced her I cared about what she said.

As her voice drifted off, the pad of my thumb ran over the typewriter letters on my wrist until I felt suffocated with pain. Coping didn't feel the same for me anymore. Those highs I used to feel are nowadays regrets, and temporary relief is tonight's reason for sitting in front of my therapist. But alcohol and fighting didn't land me here. The dickhead judge who wanted me to sit behind bars wasn't why I sat on this stupid fucking green couch as I listened to my worst mistakes from someone else's perspective.

After watching Bo walk away, I couldn't sit alone with myself. The sound of her sobs echoing through the empty street played in my head like heart strings strumming the wrong chords. So, I found myself sitting on this stupid fucking velvet green couch because I went looking for change, and I found it cooped up in a small city office.

"Why do I make her cry?" I interrupted as my head shifted to look in the lady's direction. "How is it that I wanted to give her the world, and I am the very reason it crumbled at her feet? Why do I want to do good things for her, but somehow it always goes wrong?"

She didn't say a word but let me continue as I raked my fingers through my hair. "I don't actively look for reasons to fuck everything up, but my actions are on repeat, and I don't know how to stop them from permanently playing reruns."

"Permanently playing reruns?"

"Yes," a huff shoved past my lips. "It is as if I have a shelf of movies and the only ones that get picked are the depressing movies with hours of anger and just a few seconds of happiness. I want to play her new movies, but what if my projector has been running for so long that it is incapable of being fixed? What if I cannot portray the person I want to be? Because I am fucking up, and everyone's watching as if I am on a big screen."

"What are you saying?"

The burning in my eyes made my face drop to my tattooed knees. "I am not capable of change. No matter how badly I want it or thoroughly try. Change isn't for everyone, and it's surely not meant for me."

A sigh left her lips, catching me off guard as her head moved back and forth as if I made her disappointed. "You are wrong."

I scoffed. "Enlighten me."

"You aren't capable of change, so you say," she adjusted the glasses on her face. "Then why are you here making the effort? You want to believe self-development happens just because you want to be better, and it doesn't. Either you fight through the pain, or you give up to remain the same."

"What are you saying?"

"Pick your pain because only one of those decisions will heal you, and the other will keep you up at night," she spoke gently. "You didn't walk into a gym being the best boxer; you worked for it. No matter how badly it hurt or difficult, it became, you worked until it no longer felt that way. Some things are worth fighting for, so you need to start asking if what you are fighting for is worth all of this?"

I quickly rubbed the tear from my eye before it fell. "I love her, Maleigha."

"Is she worth fighting for?"

My head started shaking. "She is worth giving up for."

"Giving up, hm?"

"I just don't want to fight anymore," my voice cracked. "And the only fight I am in is the one with myself and I constantly feel defeated."

"Why are you fighting yourself so much?"

"I want to change, but there is a small part of me who wants to walk away."

"Is that small part of you wrong for wanting to walk away?"

"Yes," my eyes met hers. "Every issue I faced, I moved forward. I am not a runner. Conflict doesn't bother me, but -"

"But?"

"I am willing to walk away from everything I know to build a life that is capable of keeping her in it," I admitted. "I never had that, so the part of me that wants to continue fighting is hard to defeat because he won't surrender."

"And what about Bo?"

"Bo never made me want to fight harder, she made me want to give up," I rubbed over my face. "One look at her, and I wanted to heal."

"She made you want to change?"

My head moved back and forth. "No, she made me want to be a better person."

"Just one look?"

"I don't believe in love at first sight," the corner of my lips tugged upward. "Don't get me wrong, but I do believe in seeing someone from across the room, and even though you don't know each other, you start to question if you'd ever be good enough for someone like that. It doesn't matter if you faced confrontation head on or that you could drop anyone with your barehands. Not at all. Because you'll look at her and realize that none of that matters. One look at her and she'll have you questioning every bad fucking decision you ever made in your life. Even though you don't know her, you're willing to change your ways just to even know her name -"

"The first time I saw her, perched on a dirty fucking couch at a random party I didn't want to be at, and she smiled, I was a fucking goner. No one kept my attention for long. Shit, my friends will tell you that ninety percent of the time, I am not listening to them, but she smiled and my eyes couldn't leave her face."

"Tell me more about the party that night," she furrowed her eyebrows. "The first time you saw her."

"Where do you want me to start?"
"From the part you can first remember."

Chapter 25

Somewhere in the neighborhood, a mom prepared dinner for her family. Not mine, though. Mine would come stumbling through the house wrapped around a stranger's body. Instead of putting food on the table, I found pill bottles and alcohol. When I should have been sitting with my family while we discussed our day, I found myself pulling a random man's body off of my mom. Sometimes I worried if I was too late and if something had ever happened to her, but I would bring the whiskey bottle to my lips to forget about it.

The more I thought about the nights I wasn't home to save my mom, the more alcohol I drank. When I realized I couldn't save her all the time, I became an alcoholic. I did whatever I could to keep my mind off the men who had the consent to be between her legs. My mom might have been too drunk to remember, but it had always been me who had to pull the covers over her body after someone ripped her clothes off.

"Is that why you struggle with Bo's situation?"

My head moved back and forth. "What do you mean?"

"You said you weren't sure if men did or did not have consent from your mom," her shoulders tipped upward. "Is that why you are so hard on Bo? You couldn't protect your mom, so you are trying to get it right this time around?"

"You haven't heard the rest," my voice cracked. "So, save your questions until the end, please."

"Okay," she nodded. "What do you remember happening next?"

It worried me when I left my mom alone. After kicking out those fucking pieces of shit she picked up at the bar, I feared they would come back. If they did, I didn't hear about it. My mom and I didn't talk, so I am not sure she was even aware of what I did for her.

After confiscating the drugs I found on the table, I would call Trevor and Miles. We would go to parties we weren't invited to, but no one ever told us to get out, especially when we had things to offer. Mom wouldn't know they were gone. Even if she did, she would find someone else to get her pills from. So, I didn't have any repercussions.

After handing off Oxycotin to an injured football player, he gave me three hundred for twenty pills. If my mom taught me anything, it was how much painkillers cost on the streets. So, the kid could play the biggest game of his career despite his injury, and I put gas in my tank and food in my stomach. It was a win-win situation.

Just as Miles was slapped in the face for accidentally spilling a drink on the girl he tried asking out, I heard a burst of laughter that caught me off guard. Trevor stood above me, laughing about our friend, but I tried finding the source of the sound.

"She looked out of place," a smile pulled across my face as I recalled the memories. "And it was beautiful really because Bo looked like she just rolled out of bed. I mean, she had a ridiculous tye-dye shirt on that looked homemade. She pulled it over her knees as they curled to her chest."

Even under the shittiest lighting, never has someone looked so beautiful. My friends would tell anyone I don't listen or pay attention to what they say ninety percent of the time. People struggle to hold my attention because most of the time, I don't really care what anyone has to say. Yet, my eyes never left that curly-haired girl.

As she laughed at what her friends said, she picked at the yellow nail polish on her toes. I wondered if she wanted to be there. Despite her smile, something made me believe she would look for any reason to get away.

My hand smacked Trevor's thigh as he laughed behind me until he answered my question. He said what he knew, though. Her name is Boston Bennett. There isn't a lot to learn about her, he said. Fuck that. After five seconds, I wanted to know everything like the stupidest shit too. What is her favorite color, and why? Does she stay up all night or go to bed early?

Just as someone stepped in front of my view of her, I shoved him forward. He continued walking up the stairs without saying anything, and just as my head turned back, I caught her staring at me. Her eyebrows were furrowed as she leaned into the blonde girl next to her, whispering something as they both looked at me.

Instead of diverting my gaze, I held contact until she looked away. It made me want to get up from my seat and ask her those questions that had been flying through my head. Would a girl like that want to talk to a guy like me? Surely I don't fit in with the people she hangs out with, but did I still have a chance?

Just as I started finding the nerve to get up, I watched someone hand her off a red-solo cup before encouraging her to drink away.

My eyes narrowed at the man in front of her as he pushed on the bottom of her cup, making her finish what he got her. As soon as the cup fell away from her lips, he leaned over her body and pressed his mouth against hers.

That is when I knew I didn't deserve her. She deserved someone clean-cut, who wore a jersey on Fridays, and came to dinner at her parent's house on Sundays. Not me. When I thought back to what happened earlier, I knew I couldn't bring her into a lifestyle like mine. The more I thought about it, the more agitation grew. Before Trevor could say a word, I got up to leave.

"That is when the wreck happened," Maleigha spoke up.

Tears burned in my eyes as I stared at the ground. "That's not the worst part, though."

"What are you talking about? What is the worst part?"

"It wasn't my mom's fault that I am hard on Bo," my voice grew heavy. "Because I was always there to pull those men off of her. If I wasn't, I never heard about it. If something happened to mom, I didn't know, but I was there to stop it."

"You couldn't stop what happened to Bo."

"That is where you are wrong."

"What are you talking about, Kinnick?"

"When I went to the kitchen to fill my cup, I watched Chrissy, Bo's friend, hand off drugs to the guy who kissed her," my voice cracked. "At the time, I didn't think anything of it. I thought she was trying to make a few extra bucks, but now knowing what I know, I was wrong."

"You blame yourself for not knowing what was going to happen?"

"I blame myself for not stopping it."

"Stopping what? You said so yourself, you weren't aware of the situation. Despite what you made yourself believe, there isn't a way of knowing what would come of that night," her head moved back and forth. "You regret the idea of not being able to save her because she has been the only person you wanted to protect.

"Despite what you had made yourself believe, there is no way you could have known what was going to happen that night," she sighed.

"I promised I would save her from everything."

"But you didn't."

My head snapped up to look at her. "Excuse me?"

"You didn't save her," she shrugged. "So, what?"

"I could have stopped her from being assaulted," I snapped. "What do you mean, so what?"

"Then why didn't you?" Her smug attitude started a fire in my chest. "You want to save her from everything, so why didn't you?"

"Because I didn't fucking know what was happening," my voice pushed harshly from my lips. "There isn't a part of me that wouldn't give my life to save hers. No hesitation. No second-guessing."

"Exactly," she nodded. "You didn't know, Kinnick. You said so yourself. You would have stopped it if you knew what would come of that night, but you didn't because you did not know. So, why carry the burden?"

"I want to believe the universe is making me screw up badly enough to push her away until it is permanent."

"And that is what we call self-sabotaging," she pointed at me with her pink pen. "Remember that when you are fighting yourself. You cannot heal if you continue being the reason you're falling apart."

"How do I know I am ready?"

"You reached out for help," Maleigha's lips tugged upward into a soft smile. "And a person who admits they need help is a person who is ready to heal."

Chapter 26

The leather deformed underneath the grip of my fingers, morphing to the curve of my nails as they dug into the surface of my steering wheel. My knuckles throbbed, and I wasn't sure if I wanted to hit something or needed to ease up on my hold. The scar tissue barely healed on my fist split, and every brush of cold air made the open wound sting. So, I rolled down the windows. I had to feel something, even if it was pain. All I need is a focus, so I don't stop this truck.

Not many bars stayed open in a small town like this one, but I didn't need to drive far if I wanted to find somewhere to drown my sorrows. Even if the doors were locked, I had the key to the most extensive supply of alcohol a single man could need. I had the keys to many things but not the curly-haired girl's heart.

My hands were curled around the rope of hope, allowing it to dangle me in the air as the pit of unknown emotions waited to swallow me. When I looked up to see why I still hung on, I swore I could see her eyes, but the burning sensation of synthetic fibers was clouding my judgment. I am unsure if it hurts more to hold on or let go at this point.

Some people say the universe sends them signs, but maybe we live on different ones. It's just that I loved her so hard I softened. If we are meant to be together, where is my sign? If the universe fights for people to be together, why does she keep getting pulled away? Perhaps it fights for people like Bo, though. I couldn't imagine why it would waste time on me. Maybe everyone was right - I don't deserve her, and she deserves better.

People also say talking through your feelings makes things more manageable, and it did for those three hours, but now I am vulnerable. Someone saw the side of me that doesn't come around often, and I feel like I have fucked up. Rarely had I opened up to Bo, but if she asked me a question, I didn't shy away or lie about it. If she were to ask me now for the truth, I would still give it to her. Because I did everything but lie to Bo.

Just as exhaustion started sweeping over me and I found myself ready to pull over, I saw a familiar golden light shining on the wet blacktop roads. As I eased my foot onto the brake, I saw a girl with her curly hair tied in a knot on the top of her head, reading from a book as she sat in an office chair.

I shifted into park before killing the power to my truck. For a while, I just sat there watching as she gently twisted back and forth in her chair with a focused look on her face. The bruising on her cheek started to dissolve, but blots of purple discolored her eye socket. Underneath the glasses on her face, a crack across the top of her nose stayed hidden.

Without hesitation, I found myself walking toward the door separating me from her. Brian sat before me, scrolling through his phone as he sat at the receptionist's desk. My head nodded toward him as I moved toward the hallway, where a little crack of light cut through the darkness.

Just as my hands slowly lifted to press the door open, her little voice broke the silence. "Brian?"

The moment we made eye contact, I noticed her reddened eyes. Something made me hope the reason for her tears had something to do with the novel in her hands, but I knew her all too well. As much as I promised to be the reason for her happiness, I became the only reason her life fell apart.

Her eyebrows pinched together as she looked up at me with genuine confusion. I knew we were both wondering why I came here, but somehow we both knew the answer. My feet carried me toward her, even though my heart begged me to keep my distance.

"What are you doing?" She whispered.

My fingers gently tipped her head backward so I could further analyze the mark on her face. She stared at me with wide eyes as her body rested on the edge of her seat. I gently brushed my thumb across the bruise on her face where stitches used to be, and a sigh exited my lips.

"I am sorry this happened to you."

"Why do you say that like you could have prevented it?"

"You act as though I wouldn't do everything in my power to keep you safe."

She turned away from me, and my fingertips grew cold from the absence of her soft skin. "What are you doing here, Kinnick?"

"I am here to make sure you have a ride home."

She pointed to the keys on her desk. "I drove."

"And I know better than anyone how you feel about driving, Bo."

As she played with her bun to readjust the fallen curls, her eyes rolled. "Stop doing that."

"Doing what?"

"Saying shit as stupid as that, thinking it will be the very reason I come tumbling into your arms again," she sighed. "It's like you don't feel; if you do, I never hear how about it."

"You don't think I am vocal about my feelings for you?"

"Not when it mattered," she mumbled. "I've spent these past few years wondering how you could love me so much but just leave?"

"You asked me to go."

"I asked you to do a lot of things, but when did you ever listen?"

A chuckle left my lips. "Never."

"And you slept with Charlie," her voice cracked. "Were you always attracted to her?"

My eyes shut gently as I sucked in a deep breath. "Us sleeping together had nothing to do with me being attracted to her, Bo."

Her teary caramels lifted from the desk to look at me. "Every time she came around, did you look at her the way you looked at me?"

"I never looked at anyone the way I look at you," I promised. "Still to this day, you are it for me."

"It hurts," she cupped her face.

I watched her shoulders slouch before her body jerked at the violent sobs leaving her lips. Once again, I found myself drawing a tally mark to keep track of how many times I made Bo cry. Before I could walk away, my body kneeled in front of her. As I tugged at her arms to gently pull her to my chest, I realized sometimes Bo needed comfort more than she needed solutions.

My fingers threaded through the bun on her head as I softly rubbed circles to soothe her. She liked when I tangled my hands through her hair, gently rubbing her to sleep as she lay on my chest. When her fingers curled around my t-shirt, I knew even in moments when I hurt her the most; she still wanted me to comfort her.

"I am sorry I didn't turn out the way you wanted me to," I murmured into her hair. "But I am trying to be all the things you loved about me, Bo."

"You don't get it," she sniffled. "Still to this day, you don't understand."

I cupped her face as she stared at me with her blotchy face frowning with heartbreak. "Then make it clear for me."

"It isn't that I want you to be a certain way," her bottom lip trembled. "It's that I love everything about you, and I am trying to figure out how not to."

"Stop trying then," I begged. "Just give in to me, Boston."

"How when you always find ways to hurt me?"

"Do you think I intend to?" My eyes stared into hers as I tried to find a lie or even the truth. "And I want your honesty. Do you think I intend to be the reason you always cry?"

"No," her eyebrows pulled together. "I don't, and it makes everything so much more confusing."

"Come home with me," I pleaded.

"If you never loved anybody, how can you look me in my eyes and know this is real?"

When her caramel eyes began to search mine, I knew what she wanted to hear, and I couldn't tell her that because she wanted me to say none of this meant a thing to me. If I wasn't the best at self-sabotage, Bo was. She would over-analyze everything she earned in life and convince herself she wasn't genuinely deserving of anything.

"Some people are worth fighting for," I mumbled. "You are worth giving it up for. I would rest my gloves and never raise my fists again if it meant keeping you around. My lips would never meet another bottle of alcohol; my soul would never know anger again. They say some people could stop wars, but until I heard your voice, I didn't know what that meant. The moment you start talking, the voices in my head stop to listen -"

"I may not have loved anybody, but I know what I feel for you isn't normal. This isn't some silly crush. My eyes only search for one person in crowded rooms. My ears only perk up at the sound of your voice. Only one girl comes to my mind when my eyes close to the moment they open, and that girl is you, Bo -"

"I slept with Charlie because I was hurting. When you said it was a mistake to love me, my world crumbled. It made me wonder why the universe wanted me to live so desperately. Overdose after overdoes, I questioned when it would all stop, but I knew as long as you were breathing, I couldn't go. I would live to make sure you got everything you wanted out of this life. So, meeting you helped me learn not everyone is to die for; sometimes people are worth living for -"

Without warning, her lips pressed against mine. I inhaled deeply through my nose, and before second-guessing what unfolded between us, my knees dropped to the ground, allowing me to sink into her. And it felt like I was dreaming. Were her hands truly running through my hair as her mouth moved against mine with such desperation?

When our lips broke apart, she was quick to ask. "Why did you come here?"

"I told you," I breathed in her air. "I wanted to make sure you had a ride home."

"How did you even know I was here?"

"Because I left my therapist's office and saw your light was on," I mumbled.

Her eyebrows furrowed as she brushed her lips against mine. "Your court-ordered therapist?"

"It just so happens she is pretty great to talk to when it comes to you."

"You talked to your therapist about me?"

"I told you I would fix the broken parts of me to keep you around."

"What if this doesn't work out in the end?"

I pressed my forehead against hers. "I will never stop trying."

"And if I asked you to?"

"You said it best earlier; I never listened."

"Don't start then."

My heart skipped a beat as her words tumbled onto my lips. "I never planned on it."

"Good."

"Come home with me, please," I begged her. "Where you belong."

"Am I going to regret this?"

"Probably."

Even after answering her question, she placed her hand in mine. In life, I knew I didn't want to go where she wouldn't follow. I would chase this woman to the ends of the earth. Wherever she went, I knew I had to go. There wasn't much searching left to do. When my head turned back to see her already staring at me, I knew I found the one thing I spent my life searching for - purpose.

Chapter 27

When Kinnick said something, I believed every word. There wasn't much he said I didn't trust. He said getting me to come home wasn't an excuse to end up in bed together, but the moment we made it to the elevator, our hands couldn't stay off one another. He walked us into the living room the second the steel doors separated. My hands steadied against his chest. The feeling of his bare skin against my palm acted as the only remedy I needed to soothe the discomfort. As we breathed in each other's air, our eyes looked into one another as if this were the last time we'd be able to see them.

My fingertips found his jaw as I struggled to find a voice inside of me to encourage the second I pulled his lips to mine. If I lost my eyesight tomorrow, I spent these short few seconds memorizing the look he gave me as our mouths mirrored each other's movements, dancing apart until finally colliding.

Suddenly our lips moving against one another weren't enough. His hands rushed for my body, yanking me closer as his fingertips dragged across the material on my body. Our lips hovered one another as a groan left his lips. He begged to touch my skin, and the clothes that held me prisoner were the only reason he couldn't touch freedom.

"Baby," he growled with desperation as he tugged at my shirt. "This needs to go."

My head moved up and down as I spoke onto his lips. "Then I don't know what's taking you so long to take it off."

I could feel his lips tugging upward, making my stomach ache for him. My nails traveled his bare back, roaming every valley and dipping into every crevice as he gripped the shirt on my body. A gasp left my lips as he ripped the material into two, stripping me free. Within an instant, his mouth fell away from mine, dragging along my cheek as he made his way to my neck. Every kiss on my skin made me whimper. Every soft bite made me melt.

As he backed me into the wall, his hands dropped to my thighs. My legs wrapped around his torso as he steadied us. The moment his body weight rested against me, I felt him. The gasp that left my lips caused him to break apart from my shoulder. My lips parted as I stared into his eyes. When his hips rolled, I felt my eyes roll back at the sensation.

"You like that, huh?" His lips found my ear as he rested his palm next to my head.

"It's not enough," I whimpered. "I need to feel you."

Without hesitation, he gripped me tightly and backed away from the wall. I held tightly onto his shoulders, feeling the scars on his skin as I gently rubbed them with my fingertips. My eyes searched his face, wondering how I could love something so much. I leaned forward, gently pressing a kiss to the scar under his eye as he carried me to the bedroom.

My back hit the comforter below me, swallowing my body with the smell of Kinnick. I didn't have time to breathe before his mouth was on mine, making up for lost time. As he pulled the shorts on my torso off, he managed to keep our lips together. The blue-eyed boxer never stopped surprising me, and as much as I hated surprises, Kinnick made me love them.

Before I could protest what he was doing, his fingers found their way to the lace on my waist. I watched as he curled his hands around the material before snapping it in half. My eyes flickered up to meet his as my lips parted in shock.

"I'll buy you another pair," he mumbled as his face fell to my neck.

"Do you promise to rip those off too?"

I felt his grin grow against my skin. "I'll do whatever you want me to, baby."

Before his fingers could travel between my legs, I gripped his wrist. "No, I need you now."

"Bo -"

"Kinnick, please," I begged with desperation. "I just want to feel you."

Maybe he sensed my desperation, and perhaps it had something to do with wanting to be enough for him after hearing that he slept with Charlie, but either way, I wanted him. As I felt him apply the pressure between my legs that I ached for, he pressed his forehead against mine to make me look at him.

As his hips rolled forward, I felt tears filling my eyes from the sensation only he gave me. My fingers ripped at the comforter as my toes curled into his back. His hands reached to cup my face, determined to hold my gaze as he continued to thrust into me. The pads of his thumbs caressed my cheeks, soothing me as my body fell apart underneath him.

His lips hovered mine, allowing our mouths to brush as he breathed in my moans and begs for more. If we weren't in love, we were making it. May the bedroom be our first chapter, and his bed our plot, but our bodies were the night sky, and this love was written for the stars.

When his forehead fell to my collarbone, my eyes shifted to watch his movements. I stared at his tattooed body, glistening in sweat through fluttering eyes, to see his hips rolling into mine. My lips parted as he continued bringing the pleasure, and I got to watch it all.

Just as I gripped his back, he rocked into me, making my thighs ripple from the impact. My head fell against the pillow, letting my nails rake down his tattoos as he continued meeting my hips with rough thrusts. My teeth latched onto his shoulder as I cried into his skin.

His shaky breath groaned against my collarbone. "Fuck, you feel so good, Bo."

My lip pouted at the sound of his voice near my ear, talking to me in the way I loved so much. "I missed you."

He pressed onto his elbows to stare at me with his blue eyes full of desperation and lust. "I missed you most."

"Prove it then."

His hands slid underneath my body, fingers curling around my shoulders as he gripped me tightly. Without warning, he rocked into me, causing the bed to creak. With every thrust, I felt the air leaving my lungs. The hold he had made it difficult to move away, but I didn't want space. He had me right where he wanted me, and I would only beg for more.

My hands cupped his face to bring his eyes back to mine. The moment his blue eyes met mine, I knew I would allow this man to have me in any way he wanted. When I first met Kinnick, I knew I would do anything to be a part of his life. Some things never change.

Just as my body tensed, his thrusts became heavier. Before I could let go, his mouth was on mine, letting me cry into him as he continued connecting our hips. He wasn't slowing down, and I wouldn't ask him to stop.

My fingers threaded through his hair, feeling the sweat on my fingers as I yanked him closer as if it were possible. While we rode out our highs, I let him breathe my screams of pleasure. Before I knew it, he was gently pulling himself from me. His hands guided me to his chest, allowing me to rest my head as we caught our breaths. As my eyes fluttered shut, his fingertips rubbed circles into my scalp.

"Are you okay? He mumbled into the stillness of the night.

My lips met his chest. "Yes."

"Good."

"What is going to happen to us?"

He hesitated a few moments before muttering to me. "I don't know, but whatever it is, I hope the universe brings us back together."

"The universe?"

"If there is a multi-verse, Bo," he sighed. "I hope we find each other in every one. I hope there is at least one where I don't constantly break your heart or give you reasons to leave. I hope in one of those universes; you'll see that I truly love you and never question it again."

"Do you think it's possible?"

"If it's not, I'll spend the rest of my life trying to get it right."

"Somehow, I always end up with you, Kinnick," I mumbled. "I don't think that's a coincidence."

"If the universe is an author, it created you just for me. Our love story would be too beautiful to end. So, it continued writing different versions to keep us alive. No matter what plot tries to break us, we will always come back to each other."

Chapter 28

The curly-haired girl favored the black t-shirt with my last name on the back. It made me wonder why. How could we be apart for so long, and moments like this, when I am watching her strut through the hallway wearing nothing but my clothes, it is like she never left? Something I learned about us is no matter where we pick up; it will be as if we never spent time apart.

The more I analyzed her, the more I realized Bo looked unhealthy. My eyes trailed down her arms, noticing they looked slimmer than usual. When I thought about the bonfire, I never saw her eat anything besides a few marshmallows. The night I brought her to the bar, she refused to eat, and at the office, I don't remember seeing anything on her desk. It made me worried she purposely began starving herself.

When I wanted to believe Bo would never do that to herself, I realized nothing was impossible with this girl. Sometimes she was as self-destructive as I was, and that fucking scared me. As I searched through the cupboards, I knew I hadn't restocked anything since she left. So, I turned to her with my arms crossed.

"How about Rosie's?"

Her caramel eyes flickered up to look at me. "It's almost six in the morning."

"What did you eat today?"

She dropped eye contact to pick at her nails. "I ate at Trevor's bonfire."

When I scoffed, she looked at me with skepticism. "What? A few marshmallows?"

"I am just not hungry, Kinnick."

With very little protest, just a little bit of huffing, she followed me to the elevator doors. If her stomach growling wasn't noticeable, how her shoulders sank with exhaustion was. Without warning, her head fell against my shoulder as she snuggled into my side. My hand dropped from the steering wheel to rub her knee as her snores filled my truck.

The way she looked made me want to turn the truck around and allow her to sleep until the next morning, but after going all day without eating, I knew I couldn't do that. I blamed myself for not paying closer attention to her lack of hunger, but as my therapist said, if I didn't know before, there is nothing I could do.

Rosie's neon sign flashed over Bo's face as I pulled into the parking lot. It would have been easier to take her through a driveway, but if she sat across from me, I could make sure she was eating. It never worried me before because the curly-haired girl devoured cheeseburgers and blueberry muffins, but something changed in her.

"Bo," my hand gently pushed at her knee. "We are here."

My heart fluttered as her eyelids twitched, slowly opening to look at me. "Well, hello."

The corner of her lips tugged upward as her caramel eyes disappeared again. "Hi."

"We are here."

Her face fell as she sighed. "I am not hungry, Kinnick."

"Please, just eat something small."

Her head moved back and forth. "I don't feel like it."

"You haven't eaten -"

"I don't know why it is a big deal; sometimes people aren't hungry," her voice got snippy.

I pushed open the driver's side door. "Come on; we are going inside."

"I had take-out," she blurted before I slipped out. "Earlier. Before I went to Trevor's."

I turned to her, leaning my hands against the seat. "Take out, huh?"

"Mhm, and it was good, so now I am full."

My eyes found hers, and I could see through the bullshit. "The closest thing you had to take out was taking my dick. Get the fuck out of the truck. We are going inside to eat."

A little gasp left her lips as she looked at me with shock. My body stepped aside, allowing her to get out. I could hear her mumbling as she climbed out behind me. The moment I heard her call me an asshole, I turned around. My chest pressed against her body, using it as leverage to shut the door behind her as I backed her against the truck. Her palms reached between us, trying to put distance between us as she tried to size me up.

"Dirty words sound so pretty coming from your lips," I pressed a kiss to her cheek. "I would love to hear you repeat yourself."

Her eyes stared up at me as the corner of her lips tugged upward. "I didn't say anything."

"You aren't a good liar, Bo."

I watched her shoulders shrug. "And you are an asshole."

Before I could process her words, she pulled me down to her lips. "Boston Bennett, are you trying to seduce me into taking you back home?"

"Is it working?" She mumbled against me.

I reached between us, shoving her gently backward. "No."

Once her eyes started rolling in annoyance, I knew she was growing upset. "Keep rolling your eyes, Bo. You can be mad all you want, but I am going to make sure you eat something."

"Whatever," she pushed away from me.

Before she could get too far, my hand collided with her ass. She flipped around, pointing at me with her eyebrows furrowed in disbelief. My shoulders tipped upward as I continued walking forward.

"I love when you give me attitude."

When I opened the door, Rosie was waiting by the register with a smile on her face. The red-lipped girl wanted to know why we were out so early, but before I could answer, Bo told her she didn't have a choice. The curly-haired girl told Rosie I held her hostage, and I am starting to think the little Delphi believed her.

I wasn't the first to believe Bo shouldn't hang around a guy like me, and I wouldn't be the last, but Rosie rooted for us. When people saw us together, they waited for Bo to look at them and plead for silent help. Perhaps she has Stockholm Syndrome, but I never held her hostage, and she still developed feelings.

As I ordered the food, Bo looked at me with disappointment. "I told you I am not eating, Kinnick."

My eyes searched the menu. "You could try."

"I don't feel good."

"How do you know depriving yourself of food isn't the reason why you aren't feeling good?"

"I should be used to it now," she murmured softly.

"Come again?" I snapped.

"What is the problem with not eating? I am a grown-ass woman, and you are not going to tell me what to do."

"Grown-ass women don't starve themselves."

"You would be surprised."

"You know what? I am surprised," I dropped the menu on the table. "How is it that you are going to fight me on this when you know I am right?"

"I don't know why you are fighting me on this."

"Name the last thing you ate besides take-out."

"Blueberry muffins."

"When?"

Her eyebrows twitched. "The day I stayed at your place."

"Exactly my fucking point," I scoffed.

A sigh left her lips as she dropped her head. "Stop getting mad at me."

"Take care of yourself and I wouldn't have to."

"I need to go to the bathroom."

Before I could say another word, she slid out of her seat. My head dropped to my hands as my fingers ran through my hair. When Bo got upset, I tried reminding myself it wasn't always my fault, but if I hurt her, I was not allowed to say I didn't. She didn't like when I called her out on her shit.

When Rosie came back with our food, I dismissed myself with the idea I would only be gone for a few minutes. The second Bo came out of the bathroom, my fingers curled around her arm to pull her toward the hallway. Her red-rimmed eyes told me all I needed to know, but it would shatter me to pieces if I watched her starve herself and not say anything.

"I am sorry," my palm cupped her cheek. "I want you to be healthy, Bo."

She frowned. "I am not feeling good."

"Baby, how do you know you aren't not feeling good because you are not eating?"

When her lip started to quiver, I could tell most of her emotions were being caused by exhaustion. "I am just tired."

"I know," my lips pressed against her forehead. "Just please eat first."

"Can we take it home?"

"If that is what you want."

"Please," she mumbled into my chest.

"I'll meet you in the truck, okay?" I put my keys into her hand.

Even when Bo didn't feel her best, she put on a smile and treated everyone sweetly. I watched the way she pulled Rosie into a hug before slipping out of the front door. When Rosie's head rolled over to look at me, I noticed the concern written on her face. She walked toward me with a speech prepared.

"Kinnick, as happy as I am to see you two together, slow down."

"Rosie -"

"After what happened between you two, you don't need to go full speed," she furrowed her eyebrows. "Babe, thinking you need to be where you want in your relationship will only make it fall apart. You have this unrealistic ideology that you should pick up where you left off, and you cannot do that."

"I don't want her to think anything has changed."

"Everything has changed," she looked at me with remorse. "Kinnick, you had time to sit with what happened to her mom. She just found out. As her parent, she isn't going to get over it easily, and you shouldn't expect her to."

"I don't want her to think I did it on purpose."

"Bo knows you didn't."

"When she found out, she thought I did it to get back at her dad."

"She wouldn't be in your truck right now if she thought you hit her mom on purpose," she pointed toward the window. "You and I both know that."

I stepped forward, pressing a kiss to the top of her head. "I love you, Rosie."

"Be slow with her, Kinnick," she pleaded. "You think you lived your life fast pace? She was raped the same night she lost her mom and had to find a way to get over both. Then to only find out that she fell in love with the reason for her mom's death and left her father on the same day. I know you were dealt shitty cards in life, but we don't compare trauma, Kinnick."

"And if I fuck all of it up anyway?"

"Not to be blunt, but you killed her mom, and she came back to you," she shrugged. "What can be worst than that?"

My hand shoved her shoulder as she let out a belt of laughter. "Tell me I am wrong!"

"I cannot stand you," a chuckle left my lips.

"I'll be right back," she smiled. "I'm going to box this up for you, real quick."

While Rosie slipped around the counter to box up our food, I slid a hundred-dollar bill underneath her cellphone. The woman would never accept it if I handed it to her, so I placed it somewhere she would find it. I turned to see her coming out with a plastic bag in her hand and a styrofoam cup.

"What is that?"

She grinned down at the cup in hand. "A to-go milkshake with extra cherries."

"The world does not deserve you, Rosie."

"You are preaching to the choir," she winked. "Drive safe, okay?"

"Do you have a ride home?"

I watched her cheeks heat up as she diverted her gaze. "Yeah."

My jaw clenched as I tried to swallow my words. "Tell Trevor not to drive stupid with you in the car because if I find out he did, I'll wring his fucking neck out."

"Get out of here," she rolled her eyes. "He lets me drive, anyway."

"Text me when you get on the road, so I can make sure I am off of it."

"Whatever, asshole," she snickered. "Love you!"

Before I opened the door, I saw Bo sleeping in my truck. I gently gripped the door handle, making sure not to wake her as I slid inside. Most of the time, Bo wasn't a heavy sleeper. It depended on how late she stayed up or if her mind started racing. I wanted to be anything but the reason she couldn't rest because I knew how much she struggled with falling asleep.

As I rested the food in between us, I waited for Rosie to lock the door. I didn't leave until I saw Trevor's car pulling into the parking lot. I often worried about her working late at night alone, but she did her best to reassure me everything was fine. It made me wonder if

Trevor has been hanging around here a lot and if I needed to talk with him to make sure he was treating her right -

"Kinnick."

My hand reached out to rest on Bo's thigh. "Are you okay?"

"Mhm," she rubbed at her eyes. "You aren't taking me back, right?"

"Taking you back where?"

"I want to stay with you."

"Your wish is my command."

"I think I missed you so much my body was restless."

"You don't have to miss me anymore, though."

"You'll leave me this time," she yawned as her eyes began drooping. "I am too much to carry, and one day, you are going to realize that."

I eased on the brake to stop at the red light. "Boston Bennett, these arms trained their whole life to carry you."

"You don't think you'll get tired?"

"I am a boxer, baby," my head rolled over to look at her as she stared at me with the caramel eyes I loved so passionately. "It isn't in my blood to get tired."

Chapter 29

The ringing from my bedside table wouldn't stop until I made it, yet I stayed still. Even when the sun cast upon my face, begging me to acknowledge its light, I squeezed my eyes shut tighter. I refused to wake up and find the spot next to me empty again. Perhaps I will fall into a deep sleep again where I only wake up to her voice. Until then, I couldn't be bothered.

I never knew fear until I met Bo. The way I couldn't sit still until I knew safety tucked her into bed at night drove me mad. If my heart is made of glass, she held it with clumsy hands, and I still trust her. She could juggle it and toss it into the air; my breath would never falter. It wasn't until I refused to wake up because I feared I wouldn't see her beside me that I started to question everything. How could I deny it? I finally found love.

My hand smacked around the bedside table until I found my phone. When the weight on top of my body stirred, my heart fluttered. I opened my eyes to see a curly-haired girl clinging to my side. Her breath fanned across my neck as she shifted, and I could hear every little snore leaving her lips.

As I found my lock button, I forced the sound from my phone to stop. I didn't want to wake her. If I did, I worried she would leave again. So, I brought the device to my ear, hoping to put an end to the person who continued calling. Before I could say a word, John's voice came through. Just as everything started to go right, he asked me to start training today. If I wanted to take the fight in Vegas, I wouldn't have a choice. I haven't trained in over two years, and if I didn't start now, I wouldn't have had preparation.

Every time I had Bo, I had to let her go again. A sigh left my lips as I ended the phone call. As much as I hated to leave the woman next to me, fearing she wouldn't come back if I told her I had to go, I knew John was right. Would she want to go? It made me wonder if Bo wanted everyone to know we were on the verge of becoming something again. What if she were embarrassed to be seen with the man who killed her mom?

I wouldn't know what to do if we gave this another shot only to figure out we should have stayed apart. Yet, sometimes when things are real, there is no denying it. My whole life, I have been unsure, though. Yet, this time, without question or second-guessing, I wasn't. Bo was my person, and nothing could change my mind about that.

My eyes fell to the curly-haired girl to see her caramel eyes staring at me. The corner of her lips tugged upward as she let out a small yawn. My lips pressed against her forehead as her body pressed deeper into mine, making me regret telling her I had to end this before it barely started.

"Good morning," her cheek snuggled into my chest.

My fingers ran through her hair as I gently rubbed her scalp. "Did you sleep okay?"

"Mhm," she hummed. "Better than ever."

"I don't want to cut this short, but I need to get up."

Her arm slowly pulled away from me. "Okay."

"You can stay here and rest if you want," I pressed myself onto my elbow to look down at her. "I can bring you back something to eat."

"Can I go with you?'

"You want John to know we are talking again? He will end up telling everybody."

Her shoulders tipped upward. "I thought it was pretty obvious we couldn't stay away from one another."

The reassurance she hit me with made the voices in my head disappear. "Then it's settled then."

"I'll be back," she pressed a kiss to my shoulder. "I need to use the bathroom first."

"I'll meet you in the living room."

She turned back to me as she slipped from the bed. "See you soon."

"Don't keep me waiting to long."

A chuckle left her lips. "As long as you promise the same."

My pinky raised into the air as I watched her smile at me. Before she disappeared around the corridor, she lifted her pinky toward me. A sigh left my lips as I tried to imagine what life would be like without her, and suddenly, I couldn't picture myself being alive without her.

I flipped the blanket off my body before finding something decent to wear from the closet of clothes I failed to wash. Maybe somewhere in this duffle bag of mine, I could find something worth a shit. Just as I heard the sink running from the bathroom, I finally remembered what it was like to not be alone in this empty apartment.

Within minutes, I heard footsteps padding on the wooden floor. My curious eyes tried to find her as I slipped into a t-shirt. When I failed to see her, I snatched my bag from the ground to follow. The once curly hair was tied into a braid down her back, revealing the top she wore. My last name spread across her shoulders, but she tied it above her waist. I always adored seeing her in my clothes.

She adjusted the strap of her shorts as she slipped into a pair of sandals. Somehow I found myself watching her more than I did getting ready myself, but I couldn't help it. After two years apart, I couldn't keep my eyes off her. Especially when I could barely see her through the sun casting down through the windows. The sun made her appear blurry. My eyes only got worst, and if I didn't take moments like this to stare at her, I might not ever remember, and I don't want to live in a world where I cannot recall every detail of her face.

When we slipped into my truck, I knew I couldn't let another day go by where the girl next to me didn't eat. She didn't protest as I pulled into the driveway of our favorite place. I could see the sadness in her eyes as she looked at the blueberry muffin, but she nibbled from the top without saying a word. My hand rested on her thigh to gently rub circles into her bare skin to show her how thankful I was. I knew if I said anything, she would resist eating, so I kept silent.

I pulled in front of the gym, turning to Bo as I parked the truck. "Are you sure you are okay with this?"

She nodded gently. "I'll catch up on some reading."

"That isn't what I meant," I watched her face, looking for the answer. "Are you okay with John knowing about this?"

"Are we trying to keep this a secret?"

"No."

"Then I am okay as long as you are."

"Bo, I am not trying to keep this a secret," I promised. "I want to ensure you are okay with everyone knowing we are talking again. You know what people have to say -"

"How often have I told you I don't care what other people say? I remember at one point you didn't either."

"What people say about me doesn't matter," I shrugged. "I worry that it will get to you. I don't want you to hear it and think everyone is right."

"It used to bother me, but not anymore."

"Then we have nothing to worry about."

She slipped from the passenger seat, waiting for me as I grabbed my duffle bag. As I walked toward the door, her hand reached out for mine. I looked down at her desperation to tangle our fingers, wondering if everything was okay as she promised. Her head rested against my shoulder as we walked in together.

Before I had the chance to ask if something was wrong, John came down from the ring with a smile on his face. I narrowed my eyes at him, hoping he would realize I was asking him not to make a big deal of this.

"Bo," John gushed. "I missed you!"

A giggle pushed past her lips as she fell into his arms. "I missed you too."

"Am I training you for the fight in Vegas?"

She patted her bicep as she pretended to flex it. "How could you tell?"

"I know a fighter when I see one," he teased. "Make yourself comfortable, Bo. My office is open if you want to sit there for a while."

She pressed a kiss to his cheek. "Thank you, John."

As she walked away, he turned to me with wide eyes. "Shut the fuck up."

"What? I am excited to see you two together."

My eyes rolled. "Don't start. I don't want to overwhelm her."

"Get your hands wrapped," he pointed down at me. "It's time to release some of that anger."

As Bo found a comfortable position on the table across from the ring, I covered my knuckles in the black cloth the protect myself. I watched as she pulled a book from her purse, yawning as she spread the pages over her lap. Without warning, John's pad collided with my head.

"Pay attention."

My eyes narrowed at him. "Do not hit me again. I will drop your ass without hesitating."

"How are you going to win if you cannot focus?"

My hand pointed toward my girl. "I am making sure she is comfortable."

John turned toward the curly-haired girl. "Bo? You are okay, right?"

Her eyes left the book to lift into the air. "Uh-huh. All good."

My shoulds relaxed at the sound of her voice. She hurried to drop her focus to the words printed onto the pages below her. The corner of my lips tugged upward. Bo hated nothing more than being bothered while she was trying to read. So, it made it easy when I needed to train.

John looked at me with his pads in the air, asking me to hit him. With every strike, I felt the release of anger. All of the sadness from the past two years slipped away as I ducked my trainer's blows.

As the sweat poured down my face, I continued doing as John said. It made me realize how out of shape I was when it came to moments like this. I worried I wouldn't be ready for the fight, but I knew I would do anything to make sure I was. I refused to lose.

When the clock above us buzzed, my arms dropped. John asked me to breathe deeply through my nose and follow with an exhale through the mouth. I needed to focus on the amount of air entering and exiting my lungs if I wanted to prevent myself from getting winded. It would lead to a knockout or an easy win for him, and I couldn't let that happen.

Just as I reached for my water bottle on the side of the ring, I noticed the curly-haired girl disappeared. "Where the fuck did she go?"

John searched the floor. "I don't know -"

"Bo?" My voice boomed through the room.

I slid out of the ring, searching the hallway for her. When I called out her name, I didn't hear a response. It made me worry she left without saying a word. My fingers ran through my hair as I turned to John for an answer I knew he didn't have.

"John, where the fuck is she?"

"Kinnick, she wouldn't have left without telling you."

"I didn't even fucking see her move from that spot," I pointed at the table. "How am I supposed to know she wasn't trying to tell me?"

"You wouldn't ignore her -"

"Are you looking for Bo?" A guy spoke up. "She went down the hallway."

The second the words left the random mans lips, I rushed toward the corridor. With each door I pushed through, I started to lose hope. When my head snapped to the side, I could see a small light coming through John's door. The glass showed me the curly-haired girl curled up in a desk chair with her knees tucked to her chest.

My back fell against the wall as I dropped to the ground. She slept peacefully at his desk with her book rested over her lap. When I noticed she was gone, my heart stopped. I don't know why I wasn't paying attention. Anything could have happened, and I wasn't pay-ing attention.

John came around the corner. "Kid -"

"I thought she left again."

"She wouldn't do that again."

"It has happened several times already," my voice cracked. "It gets easier every time she goes."

"Well, you did kill her mom," he pats my thigh as he joins me on the ground. "It wasn't on purpose. We all know that. Except, Bo didn't, and she took in a lot of information the night everything came out."

"She started seeing someone else -"

"You slept with her best friend's cousin."

"It wasn't the best friend she told me not to worry about."

"Kid," he sighed. "Despite everything, you're going to love her, right?"

"Of course, I am going to love her, John. What kind of question is that?"

"Everyone reacts differently," he looked at me. "You can't hold any of that against her if you don't want her to hold the death of her mom against you."

Chapter 30

W hen the streetlights cast through the windshield, I could see her face. Her cheek rested on my thigh as little snores left her lips. It didn't matter how often I expressed my concerns to Bo; she would fall asleep with her head resting on my lap while I drove. To soothe my nerves, I would run my fingers through her hair. I knew if anything happened, I would protect her at all costs.

The words John said continuously played in my head. They distracted me enough to miss my exit twice. How could I not treat her differently? I ripped her heart out and watched everyone kick it around. When I promised to be different, I hurt her worst.

I didn't know she would fall in love with me, though. I never thought she would talk to me, and the moment she showed up to school with homemade blueberry muffins in a paper brown bag to make sure I ate breakfast that morning was insanity. Things might have been different if I knew then what I know now.

Maybe it wasn't her sleeping with Luke that hurt me because I did the same thing with different women. Perhaps I hated the idea of someone proving to Bo there was more out there for her than me. It is why I gave him shit in class and snapped at him every chance I got. Before I knew what happened with Warren, I couldn't understand why she wouldn't want a clean-cut boy who played on the football team like him. Until this day, I will continue asking why me.

I never wanted to give myself to someone. When people asked me to get better, I didn't have a reason, and I sure as fuck didn't feel like I needed to. I felt comfortable being the piece of shit everyone made me out to be.

Then I saw her at the front door of John's gym, and for the first time since my dad, I felt scared. The girl I struggled to forget about from that party years back was standing in front of me, and suddenly, I hated everything about myself. How could I erase the past? How could I be good enough for her to want me around? Bo has made me question every little fucking thing in my life and -

"Kinnick," her voice silenced the ones in my head.

My fingers brushed the curls away from her face. "Are you okay?"

"Mhm," her little hum filled my truck. "Are we almost home?"

"I am pulling in now, baby."

"What if I am too tired to walk?"

"What do you mean?"

"I don't think I can walk inside."

"You thought I was going to let you?" I pulled into my parking space. "I already planned on carrying you in, Bo."

"Really?" Her face turned to look up at me.

My lips slowly started curving upright. "Really."

Instead of allowing me to carry her in my arms, she asked me to climb onto my back. Her head rested against my shoulder as I firmly gripped her thighs. With the exhaustion she felt, I feared she would fall. After promising to keep her legs around me, she fell asleep again. As she did every time, her body went limp against me.

As the elevator doors separated, I walked her to the bedroom. She didn't hesitate to curl into the sheets. The muscles in my body told me to climb in next to her, but I couldn't let Bo fall asleep without eating again.

While I prepared spaghetti for the curly-haired girl, I started cleaning up around the apartment. I knew Bo would wake up thinking she had to clean, but I wanted her to rest, so I did it for her. From wiping down the counters with her favorite lemon-scented cleaner to starting a new load of laundry with the scent boosters she used too much of, I tried to do everything similar.

"What are you doing?"

As I rested a washrag over my shoulder, I saw Bo leaning against the doorway. "I am making dinner."

"Aren't you tired?" I watched her expression change.

"I am fine."

"I'll finish cooking," her head moved back and forth. "Go take a shower."

"Bo -"

"I wasn't asking, Kinnick," she pointed toward the hallway. "Go take a shower."

My teeth sunk into my bottom lip as I watched her with amusement. "You are being quite bossy, Miss Bennett."

"Only because you are so stubborn, Kinnick Carson."

I stepped toward her, letting my fingers grip her hip. "How about I finish cooking, and we can take a shower together?"

Her face screwed up in disgust, making me wonder if I should let her cook instead. "Were you using the lemon cleaner?"

"I knew you liked it."

The expression on her face lifted as she looked up at me with pure happiness. "How?"

"Because my apartment didn't start smelling like lemons until you moved in," I chuckled. "Plus, the top item on every grocery list you ever gave me was lemon-scented disinfectant wipes."

A giggle left her lips as she rested her forehead against my bare chest. "I didn't realize I did that."

"That is the thing," I kissed the top of her head. "I notice everything about you, Bo."

Her arms tightened around my waist. "I love you."

The amount of air entering my lungs made them burn. "Really?"

She pulled away from me. "Of course."

"I love you," my palm cupped her cheek. "More than I think you'll ever know."

"If you loved me, you would take a shower so I could cook you dinner."

A rumble of laughter emitted from my mouth. "Way to ruin a sentimental moment."

"It would have been sentimental if you didn't stink."

"I stink?" I lifted my elbow to shove my armpit in her face. "Are you sure?"

She shoved away from me. "You are disgusting!"

"Get a good whiff, baby!"

Her hands pressed against my chest. "You need serious help."

"I'll be out soon," I kissed the top of her head once more.

Before I could leave the room, her voice called out for me. "Did you buy cheese?"

"Did I buy cheese?" I scoffed in disbelief. "I fucking stocked my whole shelf in the fridge because I know you can't eat spaghetti without it."

She struggled to fight her smile. "You have my heart."

"And I will always keep it safe."

Her pinky raised into the air. "Promise?"

"I pinky promise."

Chapter 31

The woman beside me fixated her gaze on the Harry Potter movies. I wasn't sure which one we were watching, and if I asked the curly-haired girl, she would snap at the idea I never paid enough attention to find out. I just knew it had the bitch who wore too much pink in it. How do I explain to her the movies were never as interesting as her reaction to them? I wanted to see what upset her as much as I wanted to see the very moments she started to smile.

I questioned why Bo loved this movie in particular. Whenever she saw that specific professor, her eyes would narrow. The first time I heard Bo say the word bitch wasn't because she said it to somebody, but because she said it to a fictional character. This woman is just trying to do her job, and there are a million people across the world who hate her. I guess she is doing her job right.

Bo asked me every five seconds if I loved these movies. I don't, but I cannot tell her that. I love how much she loves them, though. She thought they were the definition of cinema aside from every Marvel movie ever made. I thought they were pretty fucking genius, though.

If it made my girl smile, it was already at the top of my fucking list for the best movies to ever be created.

I nibbled on my bottom lip, fighting back the urge to laugh as I watched her mouth the lines of her favorite person, Hermoine. She adored that woman, and I adored how much she loved fictional characters. They weren't real to me, but they were real to her.

When the music started to pick up, I watched Bo's demeanor change. She watched this movie more than she had blinked, but nothing made her nerves skyrocket like watching her favorite movies. I watched as she started shoveling spaghetti down her throat, and even if it made me happy to see her eating, I worried she would choke.

"Bo, slow down," I snapped.

Just as she turned to speak, she inhaled deeply. I watched her eyes meet mine as they widened. My body shot from the couch as her fingers curled around the base of her throat. Just as my arms wrapped around her, she started panting.

"I am okay," she held up her hand. "I am sorry."

A breath of air left my lungs as I rubbed my palm over my face. "I told you to slow down."

When the pressure on my chest pushed me onto the couch, my eyes shot open to see Bo steadying her hands on my shoulders as she spread her thighs over my lap. My head fell back as I watched her gather the curls I adored onto one side of her neck before her lips came down to meet mine.

"I said I was sorry," her words fanned across my mouth.

I stared into her caramel eyes. "Your apologies are good."

A little giggle left her lips as she pressed them against me. My head fell against the backside of the couch as she dominated me.

I loved moments like this when her confidence wasn't in question, and her fingers were trailing every inch of my bare skin.

The corner of my lips tugged upward as she arched her back, allowing my hand to slide underneath her loose shorts and squeeze her ass. As she pressed further into me, I reached between her legs with my free hand to slowly drag my middle finger between her legs. My jaw clenched at the heat radiating from her thin shorts.

Her knees slipped against the couch as she tried to push deeper into my hand. She hated the way I teased her, barely touching her with my fingers. When my finger slipped in between her folds, the cloth curled around me. She wanted me to put her shorts to the side, but I loved making her beg.

"Kinnick," her palm pressed against the back of the couch as she held herself up.

I watched her face with adoration. "What, baby?"

Her lips parted as I palmed her. "I am sorry."

"Your apology is accepted," I kissed her neck.

"Then why are you teasing me?"

"I want to make sure you never do that shit again."

"If this is the price I pay, I'll do it all of the time."

When the words left her lips, I lifted her up. She barely had time to process my movements as I laid her on the couch. I didn't waste a second connecting our lips as I encouraged her thighs to spread for me. She moaned into my mouth as I dropped my hips, letting her feel the growth in my shorts.

As I reached down to pull off her shorts, her hand reached out to stop me. "Wait -"

"Are you okay?"

"I can't," she panted. "Not like this."

I furrowed my eyebrows. "What do you mean?"

"I can't tell you," her head moved back and forth. "Can we just try a different position?"

I cupped her face in between my palms. "Bo, you can tell me anything."

Her eyes squeezed shut as if she was embarrassed by what she was going to say. "When Luke and I had sex, he would get rough. He would always be on top because he liked to feel dominant."

Ice filled my veins as I watched her reaction. "Did he hurt you?"

"I am fine," her hands trembled.

"Bo -"

"Can I ride you?"

My curly-haired girl stared at me until her cheeks started to turn pink, and she started feeling embarrassed. A smile cracked across my lips because I almost started choking on her confidence. I couldn't help but shake my head back and forth as she tried clenching her thighs together.

"I would love for you to ride me," I played with her hair. "But I want to talk about what you just said."

"No," she protested. "Wait until after, please."

"Why?"

"Because we have been apart for two years," she sighed. "So, let me ride you."

"Bo -"

"Kinnick, please," she pouted. "Not right now."

I inhaled deeply as I stared down at her. "Okay."

Her head nodded as she mumbled. "How do I do it?"

My fingers trailed up her thighs, slowly searching for the shorts around her waist. The moment I pulled the thin piece of material from underneath my oversized t-shirt, her lips were on mine. My hands were back at her hips as I moved back, pulling her onto my lap.

A gasp left her lips as I used my hold to guide her back and forth over my shorts. Her nails continued to dig into my shoulders as she trembled. I broke away from her kiss to trail my lips down her neck. Just as her breathing stopped, I knew. Her teeth latched onto my shoulder as I continued to guide her hips back and forth.

"Kinnick," she panted.

My teeth nibbled at her collarbones. "What do you want?"

"You," her breath fanned against my ear. "It is always going to be you."

My heart clenched at her soft words as she pressed her face into my neck, peppering sweet kisses against my skin. The side of my face pushed deeper into her hair as I hoped to get closer to the woman I was so in love with. As I continued guiding her hips back and forth, my eyes closed gently, taking in everything. Then her eager hands started to pull down the waistband of my shorts.

"Woah, woah, woah," I chuckled. "We've got all night."

"Then we better get to the good stuff now," she pushed away from me, standing up to allow me space.

I looped my fingers through the waistband of my shorts, dropping them for her as she asked. My curly-haired girl always struggled with finding something to stare at. When I caught her hand to pull her closer to me, I noticed the pink settling into her cheeks. As her legs spread over me, warming my thighs with her own, she sucked in deep breaths.

"I've got you, okay?" I looked up at her. "Are you ready?"

Her fingertips dug into my shoulders as she pushed up on her knees. As she nodded, I positioned myself underneath her. She slowly sunk down, breathing heavily as her eyes rolled back into her head. I tried to watch her face and how beautiful she looked when she was thinking about nothing but her own pleasure, but my head fell back against the couch, and my eyes squeezed shut.

"Oh my god," her shaky voice whimpered.

"Are you okay?"

A groan emitted from my throat as she pushed up on her knees before allowing herself to sink back down. My fingers curled around her waist as she rolled her hips back and forth. This shit wasn't going to last long with the way she moved. I was about to lose my mind at the feeling of her pace speeding up.

I let my hands glide down her back before I cupped her ass in my palms. A cry left her lips as I helped her move. She clung to me, face falling into my neck as I thrust up to her. The sounds coming from her mouth made me squeeze her tighter to me.

"You feel so fucking good," I growled into her clammy skin.

Her head rested against mine. "Kinnick."

She let out a cry against my skin as I lifted her with my hands, letting my hips thrust up to her until her nails were ripping my shoulders. When my name continued to leave her lips, I cupped her face to bring her focus back onto me.

"I am right here," I promised. "I am not going anywhere."

A cry left her lips as she pressed her forehead against mine. "Promise?"

"I promise," I kissed her cheek.

When she pushed up on her knees, she slowly started to learn her own rhythm. I watched as she learned how to pleasure herself with my body, and my chest filled with pride. My fingers curled around her hips, loving the feeling of her scar underneath the pad of my thumb.

She was only using me to reach her peak. It made me the luckiest fucking man alive. When her head fell forward, I felt her teeth latch onto my shoulder. I could feel the heat of her breath on my skin as she cried out. My arms curled around her back as I pulled her closer to me. I tightened my grip as the seconds passed because I never wanted to let go, and I made the promise not to.

"I love you," she whimpered.

My lips found her ear as she tensed against me. "I love you."

Chapter 32

Our bedroom air felt thick with the aftermath of passionate love and sex. After coming down from her high, she dragged me to the bedroom, where I buried myself in her again, allowing pleasure to bloom between her legs.

She begged me to fuck her underneath the candlelight as the storm brewed outside. I wanted to give Bo everything she wanted, so I fulfilled every wish as I filled her. Her favorite scent of eucalyptus and mint filled the atmosphere around us as it disturbed the sweat created by the friction of our bodies.

As the wind whistled from the open window, cries fell from her lips. It was as if she had stopped worrying about who would hear her. The way she screamed guaranteed the neighbors would know my name; if the city didn't know me before, they do now. As long as everyone fucking knew I belonged to the most beautiful woman, that was all I needed.

Now she is pressed into my side, tightening her leg around my torso as I play with her hair. The arm propped underneath my head started to numb, but I refused to move. I didn't want to ruin this moment between Bo and me.

The cool breeze drifting through the window made her body tense. I watched her eyes flutter shut as her lips tugged upward. I couldn't help but smile at the small things that made her love life.

While the wind whistled outside, we waited for the rain to fall. Something inside of me stilled at the feeling of her hand against my bare chest. Her curls cascaded over my bare skin as she listened to the beat of my heart below her ear. I could feel the breath falling from her lips. It made goosebumps rise on my skin.

I loved how she clung to me. Her naked body against mine felt like redemption. My fingertips couldn't stop caressing her soft skin. My eyes trailed down her bare side. I couldn't stop staring at the sweat glistening on her body. Every curve appeared more defined in the candlelight. Every inch of skin glowed underneath the golden flame.

"Will you talk to me?" Her soft whisper filled the air.

My eyes lifted to look at her face. "What do you want me to talk about?"

"It doesn't matter," her eyes stayed shut as she moved her head back and forth. "I just like the sound of your voice."

My heart fluttered in my chest as I kissed her forehead. "How are you feeling?"

"Tired," she yawned into the palm of her hand.

"Why don't you try sleeping?"

"Because I would rather talk to you."

"Baby, I'll be here tomorrow," I promised. "You can talk to me as much as you like."

"I like to talk more when it's dark out."

"How about you talk to me about what you said earlier?"

A little sigh left her lips. "What part?"

"All of it."

"Why would you want to hear about me having sex with somebody else?"

I caressed her back. "Bo, if something happens to you, I want you to feel comfortable telling me about it. I don't care what it is about."

"He just got too rough sometimes," her voice got smaller. "That's all."

"No, that's not all," I tilted her chin to make her look at me. "Open your eyes, Boston."

When her caramels fluttered open, I cupped her cheek. "That wasn't okay for him to be that way with you."

"I never told him to stop -"

"That doesn't make it any better."

"After Warren, I just want to be in control," she mumbled. "I can stop whenever I want -"

"Boston," I snapped, making her eyes go wide. "You don't have to be in control. Say the fucking words, and I will stop. Every single time."

"I still get scared," she whimpered. "I freeze up."

"Have I ever made you feel like I wouldn't stop?"

"I say your name."

"What?"

She started to breathe heavily. "Every time I say your name and you pull me closer or let me know you are with me, I am safe."

"Promise me I never made you feel like I wouldn't stop?"

"I promise," she leaned into my touch. "I was just trying to search for you in other people because I made myself believe I couldn't have you."

"I am sorry for everything I have done to you," I murmured. "It was never my intention to put you through any of this."

"I know, but sometimes I could have made it easier on the both of us."

"You never did anything wrong."

"I left you instead of listening to you."

"I left you instead of trying to make you listen."

"But that's the thing I love about you, Kinnick," her eyes held my gaze. "You never made me do anything I didn't want to."

"I knew you didn't want me around."

"That is the horrible thing about it all," she sighed. "You are the only person I want to run to when someone hurts me. Who am I supposed to run to when you are the one hurting me?"

"You don't have to run anymore."

She closed the distance between us, connecting our lips as she muttered against my lips. "I love you."

"I love you."

"You have court at noon tomorrow," she rested her cheek against my shoulder. "You'll be there, right? If you miss -"

"I promise I will be there."

"I have to work, so I can't be there," her face scrunched up. "But I will meet you back here."

"Move back in with me."

"What?"

"You were going to before."

"Kinnick -"

"I don't want to be any further away from you than I am right now."

"What am I supposed to do with all of my stuff? We would never have enough room."

"I was looking at a house," I blurted. "After you left, I didn't want to come back here. So, I started searching for something else."

"A house?"

"We can go look at it," I cleared my throat as my heart started pounding. "It's about twenty minutes from here."

Her lips parted as she struggled to find the words. "Okay."

"You don't have to - I was just saying."

"I'll go with you."

"Okay," I ran my hand through my hair. "Sounds like a plan."

"Mhm," she chuckled.

"Why are you laughing?" I grumbled.

"Because you are getting so nervous," she poked my cheek. "Rarely do you ever get nervous."

"Well, curly-haired girls aren't good for my health."

"I'd say," she giggled. "Your heart is beating really fast."

A burst of laughter filled the air when I shoved her away from my chest. "Aw, don't be embarrassed, Kinnick Carson!"

"I am not embarrassed," I gently pinched at her waist, loving to see her jolt. "I want the best for you, and I don't want to fuck it up."

"Fuck it up, huh?"

"Yes. Fucking you over has been a recurring thing for me."

"You could just fuck me instead."

My head snapped to the side to see her staring at me with a smirk on her face. "I am just saying."

Without hesitation, my body rolled over to hover over hers. I watched her teeth sink between her lips as her leg wrapped around my torso to pull me closer. Bo made it clear we weren't getting much sleep tonight. As I positioned myself to slide in, her heel dug deeper into my back. I could feel the warmth between her legs against the tip of my fingers, making me wonder why she waited so long to say something.

"We'll get a noise complaint."

As she guided my forehead to rest against hers. "I don't care."

Her head pressed deeper into the pillows as I slowly filled her. "We might as well make it worth it then."

Chapter 33

My thumb caressed the typewriter lettering on my wrist. When my therapist told me to find something that would ground me, my newest tattoo became my ten toes down. The curly-haired girl told me she would be here if she could, but that didn't soothe my body from the anxiety creeping up on me.

When I spent time inside a courtroom, I never turned to see who filled the rows. I stopped counting on people to show up around the same time I realized all I would do was disappoint everyone I cared about. It didn't stop me from turning around to see if my caramel-eyed girl would be there, though.

With every empty seat, I felt my disappointment growing. The loneliness found its way back to me. Just like Bo and me, loneliness and I could never stay apart. Just as I adjusted myself to turn around, the doors opened. John stepped through the courtroom with Miles and Trevor on his side.

I watched my coach lift his hand into the air as the gavel echoed through the room. It made me wonder how they found out about my court date. I never said anything because I felt too embarrassed for anyone to hear about what I did. Somehow, no matter how badly I fucked up, they were always right there.

Sometimes you expect bad things to happen because you have become accustomed to them, but as my therapist sat on the stand, she told the judge about my improvement. It made me question myself, and if I couldn't see myself changing, was I? Yet, the blonde woman on the stand explained my breakthrough.

When the judge started speaking, I feared my therapist's testimony not to be enough. It wasn't until he issued a ninety-day probationary period that a breath of relief fell from my lips. I knew what would happen if I screwed up again before he said another word, but I didn't fear that.

I stood from the bench as the judge exited the room before turning to my therapist. "Do you believe what you said?"

"I wouldn't lie under oath, Kinnick," a smile grew on her face. "I truly would love to continue seeing you. Not only would it be beneficial for your anger, but you will need an escape when things get difficult."

"I'll call you to make another appointment."

"I'll be looking forward to it."

Just as she walked away, I saw John coming toward me. "I am proud of you, kid."

"Thank you," I muttered as he embraced me. "I am ready to let it all go."

He pulled back in confusion. "What are you talking about?"

"After Tommy, that has to be it for me."

His head moved up and down as he directed his gaze to the ground. "If that is what you believe is best."

"I won't stop coming around," I spoke. "And I won't stop inviting you over."

"None of us have been to your place," John rolled his eyes.

"As far as we know, Bo has been the only one to see it," Miles piped up.

"Fuck us, right?" Trevor added.

A chuckle left my lips. "I am taking Bo to look at a house."

"A house?" John choked. "Already? You have barely been back together for a week."

"We need a place to start over," I shrugged. "We need new memories in a place where we have room to invite everybody over."

"When are you going to look?"

I directed my gaze at Miles. "I am going to pick her up after this."

"Call us," John patted my shoulder. "I want to hear all about it."

"Thank you guys for coming," I shake my head. "I thought you didn't know the dates."

"We didn't," Trevor spoke up. "Bo asked us to be here for you because she couldn't come."

My forehead twitched as my brows furrowed. "What?"

"She is always looking out for you, kid."

"I love her," I sighed. "I love her more than life itself."

"I hope this is your forever home," John frowned. "You guys deserve happiness."

When I thought about Bo, I thought about our future. The curly-haired girl was my forever. The moment she left, I began searching for something to get away from her. When I stumbled across this house in an ad, I didn't know I would be doing the opposite of that. Then I realized the flowers growing around the perimeter made me think of her mother's garden. From the massive windows overlooking the fields of wildflowers, I knew this would be a home we could grow old in together.

While our loft is full of memories, those memories include how hard it was when we split. From the night I yelled at her for trying to aid me when Seth broke my ribs, I still found broken pieces of glass on the kitchen floor. Every shard reflecting in the light reminded me of how badly I treated her. I couldn't be reminded of that every day. I wanted to start forever if we hadn't already. After trudging through hell together, I wanted to build our own piece of heaven. I want to build us a life we aren't trying to get away from.

After parting with my friends, I waited outside of her office. It wasn't until she came down the stairs in her yellow jacket I felt calm. The way her hair was tied on the top of her head made me think about the first time we met. Except she wore hoop earrings this time. When her gaze lifted from the screen of her phone, a smile grew on her lips.

"Hi, beautiful."

Her dimple popped out as the grin deepened. "Hi."

"Come over here and give me a kiss."

Her palms rested on the leather between us as she leaned over to connect our lips. "Mmm, I missed you."

"I missed you," she squeaked.

"Get buckled up," I kissed her nose. "We have places to go and things to see."

"Did you find more than one house?"

My head moved back and forth as I pulled onto the main road. "No."

"Where did you find this one?"

"I did a lot of running outside the city to clear my head," I shrugged. "I just happened to stumble across this one. After searching for weeks, I found an ad for it."

"What made you think this is the one?"

"It reminded me of you."

After driving on the empty roads for what seemed like an eternity, I found a white house peeking out from the sea of trees. Just as I pulled onto the driveway leading up to the home, Bo watched with curiosity. When the leaves blocking her view cleared, her lips parted.

"This is it?" She turned to me with disbelief in her eyes.

I nodded. "This is it."

"Look at all of the flowers growing," she held her hands in excitement.

"I wanted it that way so you couldn't kill them."

"Kinnick," her head rolled to look at me.

"Baby," I kiss her cheek. "I am just letting you have the truth, raw."

"Are we meeting someone?"

My head moved back and forth. "No. Let's go inside."

Her wandering eyes fell on the porch swing swaying back and forth in the wind before she walked through the front door. When I heard a clap, I knew she saw the two-story windows in the living room. The sun beat down the gray wooden floors, catching the silver chandelier's surface and casting light upon the room.

"I told you I would get you the windows you wanted."

She ran her fingers along the white-bricked fireplace. Her eyes followed the stone up to the ceiling, where it ended. Without agreeing to buy the house, she was already deciding where the TV would go and what she would put on the shelves on either side of the fireplace.

"Where would we find curtains long enough for the windows?"

I shrugged. "We would have to get them custom-made."

"What am I paying for?"

"Nothing."

She narrowed her eyes. "I make good money. It is not like I am missing out on anything."

"Pay the utilities," I suggest. "I'll cover everything else."

"How much do they want for it?"

"Don't worry about it," I follow her toward the stairs that lay next to the fireplace. "It has three bedrooms. Not including the basement and office."

"Office?"

She didn't care about the luxurious stone wall bathroom or the master bedroom. Her excitement lay with the view from the bedroom window. Nothing made her happier than the backyard that never seemed to end and all of the maple trees lining the acreage. It made her smile because the leaves will turn a bright orange during the fall, and she will be lucky enough to see it every morning she wakes up.

"What do you think?"

"I think I need you to pinch me."

"Pinch you?" I chuckled.

"This is a dream, isn't it?"

"No," I promised, pulling her into a hug. "This is real-life."

"This is it," she looked around. "This is ours."

"Good," I kissed her forehead. "I already bought it."

She pushed away. "What?"

"I have something I want to show you."

She held my hand as I led her down the stairs. Her questioning mind was confused as to where we were going. We stood in front of a pale white door where I asked her to close her eyes. Her hands immediately smacked over her caramels without second-guessing me.

"On the count of three, I want you to open them," I push into the cool room.

I didn't reach two before her eyes shot open, and her body stilled. My impatient girl. She wasn't sure how to react to the room consumed by pre-lit bookshelves filled with novels. A sliding glass door led to a small concrete slab, giving light to the room.

I called her name a few times until she moved, snapping out of her trance. She walked toward the books lining the wooden shelves and ran her fingers along the spine. I trailed behind her to watch her reaction.

"Did someone leave these here?" She grabbed a novel. "I read this before."

She flipped through the pages of the dusty book. Her eyes fluttered as the whiff of aged pages drifted into the air. I watched her brows furrow as she caught sight of the inside cover. Her pouting face looked up at me with disbelief.

"These have tally marks inside of them," her eyes met mine as they welled with tears. "These are mine."

Chapter 34

The curly-haired girl sat on the couch in front of me, her legs tangled in mine as she munched on the Sour Patch Kids I bought on our way back from looking at the house. Pinched between her fingers and resting on her chest was a book that kept her attention. It made her oblivious to the amount of time I spent watching her as I thought about our future. She never agreed to move in with me, but her smile gave me confirmation before she could say anything.

As much as I wanted to stay on this couch, where I could watch her facial expressions change with every page she flipped, Trevor asked us to attend the bonfire at his house. I debated telling Bo, worried that she would be more interested in seeing Trevor than she would be roasting marshmallows.

My eyes trailed down the sweatpants covering her legs, and it hadn't been until now that I realized how small Bo actually was. She rolled the waistband at least several different times, and still, I couldn't find her feet underneath the gray material. At moments like this, I realized I wanted Bo to myself. I didn't want to share her with the world.

When she started snickering at the book in her hands, a smile tugged at my lips. She was too fucking cute for her own good. Just as her eyes regained focus on the words before her, she peered around the pages to look at me with her eyebrows pinched in confusion.

"Have you been watching me this whole time?"

My shoulders raised slightly. "So, what if I was?"

She placed a bookmark to save where she had left off. "I would tell you to stop."

"Not going to happen, darling," I cleared my throat.

Her eyes narrowed at me as if she had started piecing something together. "What is on your mind, Kinnick Carson?"

A large sigh pushed past my lips. "Trevor is having a get-together at his place. Do you want to go?"

When her arms crossed, I knew she was about to say something I didn't particularly want to hear. "Do you want to? I am kind of getting mixed signals from you. Are you asking me because you want to or because you don't want me to be upset and wonder why you never asked me to go?"

My bottom lip rolled out from between my teeth. "You are a fucking mind reader."

A smile grew on her face as she sat her book on the ground. "That is something we should keep between us. I don't need anybody learning my secrets. What kind of bonfire is this any way?"

"The kind where we sit around a fire and talk about our wildest dreams," I mocked with a cheery attitude. "Then we will roast marshmallows and wait for the stars to fall so we can make a wish."

A giggle tumbled from her lips. "This sounds like my kind of get-together."

"I know," I rubbed her knee. "That's why I want to go."

"What time should I get ready?"

"He said we should be there at seven."

"Seven?" She glanced down at the phone on her chest. "It is six-thirty! Why didn't you tell me sooner?"

"No reason."

"Kinnick," she began crawling over my thighs. "I know you better than you think. Tell me whatever is running through that pretty little head of yours."

As she crossed her arms over my chest to rest her chin on the back of her hands, I stared into her caramel eyes with worry flooding my system. "Do you like Trevor?"

Her nose scrunched up. "What?"

"You guys spent a lot of time together."

"That is what friends do."

"You and I started out like that to."

"No, we didn't," her eyes searched mine. "I looked at you for the first time and wondered what I had to do to have you around for the rest of my life. From baking you blueberry muffins to following you around the hallways of school, I knew all I ever wanted to be was somebody to you."

The curly-haired girl had a way of always being right. We were never friends, but something more complex. When she came into my life, she pranced into my black-and-white world with feet dipped in color. She added splashes of color everywhere she went, and now her footprints will forever be etched into my heart.

I knew we were more than friends when I started seeing her in everything. Blueberry muffins were no longer a sweet treat for the morning but a reminder of a curly-haired girl with a dimpled grin.

I wish for everyone in the world to have someone like Bo. She made me realize even people who didn't deserve her, like me, deserve something that makes them look forward to waking up in the morning.

I am head over heels in love with her. Fuck, I am madly in love with her. When she looked up at me, I knew I would follow her anywhere. My world will only ever revolve around her, and that is dangerous. It is lethal but true. Loving her will either destroy me or save me, but it has done both, and I am fine with either or. She could break me until my heart is left in pieces, and I would still hand it back to her.

"I love you," she pressed her lips to mine. "More than you will ever know."

"Impossible."

When she pushed away from my chest, she promised not to take long to get ready. I followed her to the bedroom. My shoulder leaned against the doorway as I watched her search through the closet of clothes she had accumulated to find something before settling on a leather jacket I hadn't seen since I picked her up from that party in the middle of the night all of those years ago.

Instead of spending too much time on her hair, she tossed it into a bun on the top of her head. I always loved when Bo put little effort into dressing up because I adored nothing more than seeing her in a pair of leggings with my t-shirt tied up on her waist.

She slipped into a pair of sandals before coming toward me. "Is this good?"

"Why do you ask?"

"Because I want to make sure I look okay."

"You will always be beautiful to me," I pressed my lips against her forehead as my arms wrapped around her frame. "Are you ready?"

"Mhm," she rested her head against my chest. "Trevor didn't ask us to bring anything, did he?"

"No, he actually begged me not to bring anything."

Her head tipped backward as she started up at me. "Why?"

"Well, we already ruined the turkey on Thanksgiving -"

A gasp left her lips. "Did he really say that?"

"No," I chuckled. "He never asked me to bring anything."

"Why do you have to pick on me?" She pushed away from me.

My palm collided with her ass as she walked past. "You are my girl. That is my job."

I watched as she flipped around, her hand ready to hit me. My fingers curled around her wrist to stop her before I backed her body into the wall. She stared up at me with wide eyes as I pinned her hand above her head.

"You didn't think that was actually going to work, did you?"

"If this is my consequence, I love getting in trouble."

My head moved back and forth. "You are wild."

"Only for you, Kinnick Carson."

Chapter 35

My caramel-eyed girl spun around Trevor's backyard. Her curly hair started slowly falling from the bun on the top of her head with every twirl. I brought the red solo cup in my hand to meet my lips, but I could never bring myself to drink the water inside because I feared the rim would block my eyesight from her.

I loved nothing more than to see her so carefree. Her golden honey skin glowed in the bonfire light as she slowly peeled away from the leather jacket. Her head fell backward as she sang the lyrics to whatever song played through the speakers.

Everyone loved having the curly-haired girl around. She knew how to spread happiness as if it were contagious, and everyone got sick from her laughter. Bo also found it impossible to stop laughing. This happens when she takes seven jello shots and plays beer-pong to prove to Miles that she can kick his ass.

As my teeth grazed the rim of my cup, I realized it had been empty the whole time. After asking Miles to keep an eye on the girl dancing before us, I stood from my seat to find something else to drink. I searched through the cooler for something other than a bottle of alcohol, only to find juice boxes.

"You guys are back together then, huh?"

My eyes lifted from the cooler to see Chrissy standing near the patio doors. "Call it what you want."

"Luke didn't hurt her on purpose," she watched as I stabbed the straw into my drink. "He was drunk."

"Bo has been around me while I have been intoxicated," I rolled my eyes. "Never one have I thought about putting my hands on her. Not unless she begged me to, anyway."

"How long until you split up again and she comes running back?"

I ran my palm over my face. "Chrissy, I don't know if you are drunk or not, but you always start shit you can never finish."

"You aren't her type, Kinnick," she sighed. "Admit it. Bo is too good for you. When are you going to realize you'll never be enough?"

I already knew that. I reminded myself every time I looked at her. "If you are trying to make a point, make it."

"She talked about getting married to Luke and having kids," she crossed her arms. "You could never give her that. You will always be the man who killed her mom."

"I am done having this conversation with you -"

"Who do you think she ran to after finding out that you slept with Charlie?" She called out to me as I walked away. "Bo was right back in Luke's bed without a second of hesitation."

"Fuck off, Chrissy."

"Remember, they always start as the friends they tell you not to worry about."

Without another word, I snatched a different bottle from the cooler. Chrissy gave me one last glance before I stepped inside Trevor's house. The cap on my beer bottle hissed as I popped it off.

Chrissy never bothered me until she started shoving the shit in my face that I think about every day. Why do people look at me and assume I don't want to settle down and have kids? I have a heart and use it, even when people think I don't.

Granted, I never worried about my future enough to wonder what it would look like until I met Bo. I never had a reason to wake up until I met her. I guess that happens when you spend your life listening to people tell you that you don't deserve happiness.

I know I don't deserve her. I never will. Why she chose me, I do not know. I wonder when she will realize I am a mistake. In the end, I hope she knows that no matter what, I always love her. Nothing mattered in my life until I met her.

Will Bo be ashamed to tell everyone that I am the father of her kids as I will proudly tell everyone she is the mother of mine? I think about it every day. Every. Single. Fucking. Day. And I will have to live with it if she doesn't want me. I have to live with never being enough for anybody, but god, it fucking hurts to know I will never be enough for Bo.

I locked the door to the bathroom, concealing me and the bottle of alcohol away from everyone. My head was in my hands as I tried to think about anything other than Bo leaving me. I tried to think about something other than Bo realizing she had wasted half of her life thinking she was in love with me.

A knock sounded at the door. "Fuck off."

The door handle jiggled before the locked door popped open. "Can you not fucking comprehend what I said?"

The light of my life stepped through the bathroom door with a credit card in her hand. Her caramel eyes drifted between me and the bottle clutched in my hand. I knew she wanted to say something, but I didn't fear she would judge me.

"Are you okay?"

I pointed at her hand. "What is with the credit card?"

"After you broke into my house that one time, I wanted to learn how to do it," she kneeled before me. "Now, answer my question."

When her hand touched my shoulder, I tried to conceal myself. The moment she called out my name, I wanted to snap. It has been difficult living like nothing phased me or hurt me because it fucking did.

Just as her hands cupped my cheeks, tears started to well in my eyes. Without another word, she pulled me into her chest. When her arms rested around my back, I felt warm salty tears fall down my cheeks.

"What happened, Kinnick?" She spoke soothingly into my ear as she caressed the back of my head.

When I didn't answer her question, she cupped my cheeks to stare at me. "Baby -"

"Why are you with me?"

She furrowed her eyebrows. "I love you."

"Have you ever loved anyone?"

"Have you?"

"Bo," the heavy breath fell from my lips. "Your mom is dead because of me, and you don't even talk to your dad anymore. I single-handedly ripped your family apart."

Her eyes stared at me like I was nothing less than the best thing that ever happened to her, and fuck, I hoped to be reading her right. "I still love you. Stop thinking you are this monster who does everything wrong."

"What have I done for you?"

"You saved me," she choked. "I was in a dark place. After what happened with my mom and Warren, I hated my life so much I don't remember there being a time I didn't think about how much I didn't want to be here. I don't remember a time when I didn't have a pen and paper in my hand as I tried putting together words that could explain why I was going to do what I wanted to do."

"Bo -"

"Kinnick without you, I would have been six feet underground. I wouldn't have realized there were other things to live for other than an abyss of depression. You saved me, and I can't thank you enough for bringing color to a world that didn't have any."

It was funny that she said that because Bo was the vivid color that filled my world. She hand-painted every petal in my garden of flowers that were wilted and bleak.

"Please, don't leave me again."

"I'm not going anywhere," she murmured into my neck as she held me. "I promise."

"I love you."

"I love you," she pressed a kiss to my shoulder. "What made you think like that?"

"It doesn't matter -"

"Did Chrissy say something to you? What did she say?"

"Nothing that I didn't already know."

"I don't care what she told you," she pushed away. "I love you, endlessly. No man could be better for me. Nobody can love me like you."

"How are you not embarrassed by someone like me?"

Her eyes widened as she debated between getting mad and being confused. "What? Embarrassed? By you? What is there to be embarrassed about?"

"I am covered in tattoos and scars. I am not clean cut."

"When did you start caring about this kind of stuff?"

"When your best friend told me I wasn't your ideal man."

"I didn't know someone else got to decide that for me," she furrowed her brows. "I want every piece of you. From the tattoos scattered all over your skin to the scars on your back, I want all of you. Forever."

"And what if we have kids? They are going to look at me and think -"

"My dad is never going to let anything happen to me," she looked me dead in the eye. "That my dad loves me unconditionally and that if everything in the world goes wrong I know I can get through it as long as he is by my side."

I blew a breath of air through my lips as I tried to keep my emotions at bay. "You would want kids with me?"

"As long as you are involved, I want it all."

"I love you is a weak way to explain what I feel for you."

"I was thinking the same thing," she gave me a heart-filled smile. "But I love you, Kinnick Carson."

I stood up, wrapping her in my arms, hoping she could feel how my heart beat when she was around. "I love you, Boston Bennett."

She leaned back in my arms, smiling up at me. "It doesn't get better than this."

It could never get better than knowing the person I loved most in this world loved me back. After spending years concealing my feelings, I could finally show how I felt. Bo never judged me. She proved to me that my feelings were valid. I could never thank her enough for allowing me to feel safe enough to open up.

"I've gotten myself into a sticky situation," she mumbled into my chest.

"What are you talking about?"

"I told Trevor and Miles I could kick both of their asses in beer-pong," she winces. "I can't do it without my better half."

I grinned down at her. "I guess it is time for the Butt Kickers to get back at it."

She bit her lip as an electric smile lit up her face. "Let's go do what we do best."

"What is that?" I tugged her into my side, looking at her with confusion.

"Prove everyone wrong."

Chapter 36

- -

After sinking the winning shot, Bo pointed at Trevor with laughter bursting from her lips. Not long before we started a new game of beer pong, Bo forgot all about our conversation in the bathroom. By the time we came back, Chrissy had fled. My caramel-eyed beauty had drunk too much to truly comprehend what had happened. When morning comes, I hope she forgets all about it. Something told me I never would.

Chrissy's words would haunt me before I laid my head down tonight. I wouldn't be able to close my eyes without replaying how I'll never be good enough for Bo as if I didn't already. My curly-haired girl promised she loved nobody more than me, but what if Chrissy was right? What if Bo ran straight to Luke after hearing I slept with Charlie? Would she do that even after he hurt her?

I leaned down into Bo's ear, promising to be back after soon. She pressed a kiss to my cheek before I left her behind to make fun of Trevor for losing the game of beer pong. My hand raked through my hair at the idea of Bo sleeping with Luke. She told me nothing more serious happened between them, and now I wonder if any of that had been a lie. The curly-haired girl had found it difficult to tell me the truth in our past, so why would she start telling it now?

I raked my hands through my hair as I left the backyard. The wind drifted through the leaves, bringing a calmness to the air around me, but I couldn't shake the feeling causing my heart to flutter.

I never worried about someone lying to me because I never cared enough about anyone to be affected by their inability to tell the truth. Now I am pacing Trevor's front yard as I light the end of a cigarette, wishing for nothing more than the feeling in my chest to go away because I finally met the person who made me question everything in life.

"Kinnick."

I brought the cigarette away from my lips as I turned to meet the eyes of the woman I loved most in this world. "Hi -"

"What did you run away for?" Her eyes fell on my hand. "I didn't know you started smoking."

"Yeah," I clenched my jaw, swallowing harshly as I stared at the ashes falling to the ground. "It's a bad habit I can't learn to break."

"Let's get out of here, yeah?"

"You are having fun -"

"At the expense of your happiness? No, thank you," her fingers gently curled around mine. "Let's go home."

Without saying another word, I let her head me to my truck. She climbed into my driver-side door, unable to disconnect our hands as she encouraged me to slide in next to her. It wasn't until I started the car that our hands finally separated.

"Do you want to talk about what's going on?"

My fingers tightened around the steering wheel. "Not tonight."

"Did I do something wrong?"

"After finding out about Charlie, did you sleep with Luke?"

"Do you think I did?"

"Please, answer me -"

"No," she turned in her seat to stare at the side of my face. "Do you think I went back to Luke after finding out about Charlie?"

My head moved back and forth as a lump grew in my throat. "No."

"I went to my office," a heavy breath fell from her lips. "I couldn't go back to Trevor's apartment without thinking about Charlie, and I couldn't go back to my apartment because I didn't want to relive everything that Luke did to me."

"Chrissy said you talked about kids and marriage with him -"

"With who? Luke?" She choked out as if she was trying to figure out if I had been telling the truth or not. "God no, Kinnick. We slept together, and then I would kick him out of my bedroom. I was a different person after everything happened. I started drinking, and I felt angry all of the time. Luke knew he only lived in my apartment to give me what I wanted before anything happened. Nothing more. Nothing less."

"What made it stop?" I asked, afraid I wouldn't want to know the answer. "Why did nothing else happen between you two?"

"I don't want to talk about it," a stutter broke up her sentence.

"Bo -"

Her face fell into the palm of her hands. "I can't talk about that with you."

"Bo, you can talk to me about anything," my fingers rubbed over her knee. "And you don't have to be embarrassed."

I watched as she slowly shifted her legs away from me before her head rolled to look out the window. "He got too rough sometimes."

"Physically?"

"He used to leave marks on my wrists," her voice sounded defeated. "I found bruises on my hips where he would pin me down."

"During sex?"

"It made my nightmares worst." I watched her hands start to shake before words fell from her lips again. "When I closed my eyes, all I could feel was Warren again. When I opened them, I saw Luke holding me down to get what he wanted, and I couldn't separate the two. So, I stopped inviting him to my room. When it got to the point where he wouldn't stop asking, I would wait at my office until he went to bed."

"How did you know he was asleep?"

"Miles."

"He didn't question what was happening between you two?"

"Miles and I barely talked after everything happened," she stared down at her lap. "I felt more betrayed by him when I found out he knew what happened to my mom. He was the first person I told about Warren. I thought I had found a genuine friend. I trusted him."

"I am sorry for being the reason you had nobody left."

"I am not," her head moved back and forth. "It made me realize that the people closest to me are the most capable of breaking me. I hadn't felt pain like that since my mom died because I hadn't loved anyone as much as I did her. It made me realize I was capable of loving someone again, and if they could hurt me as badly, perhaps they would love me too."

"You are the person I love most in this world, Bo."

"It is scary because I could say the same thing."

"Why are you afraid of that?"

I listened to her voice crack in the still of the night as she spoke out. "Because you could shatter me, and every piece would still be for you."

Chapter 37

John's voice floated through the gym as he paced the floor, flipping through paperwork on his clipboard and talking about my future. He begged me to focus. I had to make up for years of being absent in a few weeks. Somehow knowing the consequences of ignoring him didn't affect me. My thoughts would always drift back to the curly-haired girl.

After the conversation in my truck last week, silence settled between us. Bo didnt say anything I didn't already know, but I wanted to hear something sober Bo would never admit aloud. Nonetheless, her story stayed the same. Luke got too rough during sex, and no one cared enough to notice the bruises on her body.

When she spoke out about her past, I feared it would put her back in the same situation we always found ourselves in - Bo refusing to open up and her pushing everyone away. This time, it did the opposite. I found the curly-haired girl touching me in any way she could. Rather it was brushing our knees together or her fingers playing with mine, she clung to me in a way she never had.

I realized I didn't want space. We weren't close enough if her legs weren't spread over my thighs as she sat in my lap with her head pressed against my chest. In those moments, I realized I never wanted to be any further from her. Every inch of skin had to be touching. I refused to settle for anything less.

Despite her constantly clinging to me, Bo still felt embarrassed by what had happened. No amount of alcohol could give her the courage to speak about it. It made me realize Bo trusted me enough to say something when she was sober. Perhaps, I feared her lies, but I questioned the moment I realized Bo trusted me enough to tell me everything; I just had to give her the time.

My forehead fell against the leather bag as my arms collapsed in exhaustion. For the last few days, I spent every minute of my free time packing. From slowly moving boxes to the house, the apartment I shared with the curly-haired girl started becoming more empty. Although she failed to give me an answer, she couldn't stop her toes from curling when we talked about spending our first night in the new house.

A hand rested on my shoulder. "Kinnick, are you doing okay?"

My head started to shake as my eyes slowly shut. "I haven't got much sleep."

"What's going on?"

"I am trying to get everything packed," a sigh left my lips. "Bo still hasn't given me an answer about the house, and Chrissy said some shit I can't get off my mind."

"Why are you waiting for an answer from Bo? She would tell you if she didn't want to move in with you."

"I'll repeat myself since it wasn't clear before; Chrissy said some shit I can't get off my mind."

"As in?"

"I'll always be the man who killed Bo's mom."

"Kinnick -"

"It's true, John," I struggled to regulate my breathing. "If she isn't giving me an answer about the house, she is already planning on leaving me, isn't she?"

"Or she isn't giving you an answer because she never thought she had to."

"What is that supposed to mean?"

"You only want validation because of what Chrissy said," he tapped me with the clipboard. "We already know Bo is dying to decorate. I guarantee she has a spot for the Christmas tree too."

A snort left my lips because only last night had the curly-haired girl been online searching for the perfect Christmas tree. She begged for cashmere tips dipped in silver glitter, promising to clean it up as if I cared about any of that. Bo never had to beg for what she wanted; she just got it. I don't know why she questioned me. She knows I would never lie, so I don't know why she struggled to understand when I told her I would give her everything her heart desired.

Before I could say a word to John, my phone started ringing. I reached into my pocket to pull out the device with my curly-haired girl on the screen. As I slid the answer button, I brought it to my ear.

"Hi, pretty girl."

Her soft voice soothed any discomfort in my muscles. "Hi, Kinnick."

"Are you okay?"

"I just missed you," her voice became heavy. "I wanted to make sure you weren't pushing yourself too hard."

"I'll be home soon, okay? Do you want me to pick something up for dinner?"

"Actually, I was kind of hoping you would meet me at the new house."

My eyebrows furrowed in confusion. "For any reason in particular?"

"The furniture is being delivered, but the company told me you would have to be present to accept the order."

"Of course; I'll be wherever you need me."

"Then I don't know why you aren't at home yet."

"Soon," I promised. "I'll be home soon. I love you."

"Until then, Kinnick Carson," she mumbled. "I love you."

Shortly after ending the phone call with Bo, John dismissed me for the night. He asked me to take an early day to spend the rest of it resting. It hadn't been until I slid into the driver's seat of my truck that I realized how exhausted my body was.

When my truck finally hit the gravel road leading to our home, I unbuckled from my seat belt to meet Bo inside. Before I could reach the first step, the front door flew open. My curly-haired girl launched off the porch. Her body collided with mine as she wrapped her arms around my neck.

A hiss left my lips at the pain flaring through my body, catching Bo by surprise. "Are you okay?"

"A little sore," I winced. "Everything is okay."

She untangled her arms from my neck. "I am sorry -"

My grip tightened around her waist as my face pressed into her neck. "That doesn't mean I don't want to hug you. It has been eight hours. I missed you, Bo."

"Do you want to go inside?"

My fingers slid down her arms until they were tangling with her hand. "Let's go, baby."

Just as I pulled the front door open for her, my eyes immediately noticed the living room. "Wait - when did you do all of this? I thought the furniture couldn't be delivered."

"Thanks to Miles and Trevor, they moved the bigger stuff," she shrugged. "Rosie and I went shopping for small stuff."

"Small stuff, huh?" My fingers pinched at the velvet gray curtains. "Where did you find these?"

"They were pretty expensive," her nose scrunched up. "It's okay, though. It was a friend of Rosie's."

"It looks great, Boston," I pressed a kiss to the top of her head.

"I bought a new bed," she blurted. "I remember you saying the old one hurt your back too much, and I didn't want you to spend every night training to come home and sleep on a mattress that doesn't help you sleep -"

"Calm down," I brought her into my arms. "It's okay."

Without warning, I knocked her legs out from underneath her. A smile tugged at my lips as her laughter filled the house. This woman never stopped surprising me, and at moments like this, I realized I would never stop falling in love with her.

"Thank you," I murmured to her. "For everything."

"I know how badly you wanted to move and get everything finalized."

"Not as badly as I wanted to know if you were moving in with me."

"Why wouldn't I? I don't want to be any further from you than I am right now."

"Me neither," I kicked open our bedroom door. "Holy shit. A king?"

"We needed more space -"

"For what?"

"Well, what if I plan on getting a dog or something? He will need room to sleep."

"Bo, please," I snorted.

She let out a squeal as I tossed her onto the silver comforter. "Kinnick!"

When I fell back onto the mattress, a sigh left my lips. The comfort swallowed me whole, and suddenly I felt weightless. Whatever Bo wanted, I trusted. So, when she told me about her newest purchase, I wasn't worried.

"This is perfect," I muttered.

My eyes squeezed shut as her lips touched my forehead. "Anything for you."

"Come here."

Without hesitation, she snuggled into my side as I played with her hair. My fingertips rubbed circles into her scalp while she held me tightly. Her fingers curled into my shirt as she mumbled into my neck.

"Guess what."

I pressed my lips to her forehead. "Hm?"

"It's our first night in the new house."

A chuckle left my lips. "Yes, baby. It is."

When someone asked me what I wanted to be when I got older, my answer always remained the same. I grew up wondering when people would stop expecting my only goal in life to change. The only thing I strived for in life was happiness. I only ever wanted to be happy. Looking down at the curly-haired girl cuddled into my side made me realize I found it, and I would be dammed if I let it go.

Chapter 38

The sound of Bo crying out my name awoke me. My back lifted from the mattress as the darkness of our room consumed me. I reached out to find the curly-haired girl, but my palm collided with the empty space beside me. As I slipped from the comforter, her cries continued filling the air. My eyes searched the hallway, but I could hear her sobs below me.

I flipped the lights on as I hurried down the staircase to find Bo sitting on the couch. Her face hid between her knees as her body violently started to shake. The confusion filling my veins made me question when she slipped out of bed. Rarely had Bo been able to leave our bedroom without me realizing it.

The caramel eyes I adored so much opened to look at me. The terror in her eyes would haunt my dreams forever, but before I could question why she had been crying, her arms shot out for me. My body collided with the couch as tears soaked my shoulder. Her grip tightened around my neck as sobs racked through her body.

I caressed her skin, hoping to soothe every ounce of discomfort she felt. My lips pressed against the top of her head. My lips touched her ear as I softly whispered promises to keep her safe.

"Bo -"

"I can't remember," she choked. "I can't fucking remember."

My eyebrows pulled together in confusion as I looked over her face. The horror written into her expression was evident, but I questioned what caused it as she sat on my lap, telling me she couldn't remember something. Her eyes swelled from the tears that would never stop falling, and they crushed me as much as they confused me.

"What can't you remember, baby?"

"The party," she raked her fingers through her hair. "I can't remember the party."

"You are having dreams again?"

"I've had them ever since we split up."

My shoulders fell in defeat as her head fell against my chest. As my palms felt the vibration of her violently shaking below me, I felt the guilt eat away at my consciousness. As the girl below me fell apart, I knew I could never fill the hole in her heart. Nothing could fill the cracks broken by the man who claimed to love her.

"Maybe you should talk to somebody," I murmured into her hair.

She pushed away from my chest. "Like a therapist?"

"Yes -"

"After what happened with my last one, though, I can't."

"Baby, you tried to do something that could have cost your life," I cupped her cheeks. "The circumstances are different this time."

"What if it doesn't work?"

"Then it doesn't work, and we try something new."

"Just like that?"

"Just like that," my forehead rested against hers. "It can be as easy as you want it."

"I can call around in the morning."

"I'll be here the whole time."

I breathed the same air as her, and it brought me comfort. When she inhaled, I felt my lips dry with the cold air. Just as she exhaled, the warmth brought me back to life. At the moment, it felt as if I only survived off the air she provided me. It had been true regardless. Bo had been the air in my atmosphere, for she was the only thing giving me life.

"I need to remember what happened that night."

"What if you can't?"

"I have to," her words rushed out.

"I'll help you anyway I can."

"I love you."

A chuckle left my lips as I kissed the tip of her nose. "I love you."

"Not as much as I love you."

I wanted to tell her how impossible that was. The woman sitting on my lap hadn't known the feeling inside my chest and how it amplified every time she was near. She would never understand what she has done for me. The curly-haired girl is oblivious to the difference she made in my life. I am a better man because of it.

"You would have loved me more if you knew me before everything happened."

"Why?"

"I laughed more," her shoulders tipped upward. "I was happier then and carefree."

"I love you now."

"But you understand -"

"I don't need to," my head moved back and forth. "I love you now. I fell in love with the woman you are, not the woman you used to be. Would I love you regardless? Yes. But I love you now."

"I can't let go of who I used to be."

"I know, baby," I kissed her shoulder. "You might think everything is dark right now, but how do you think seeds feel? We pile dirt on top of them and drown them in water. And still, they grow."

"It isn't that simple, though."

"You're right," I nodded. "But whoever said it was simple being a flower? It never knows the weather or the circumstances in which it will grow, so they are vulnerable. Yes, in the winter, they die, but they come back in the springtime to sprout all over again."

"What are you trying to say?"

"You are like a flower, Bo," I laced our fingers. "You have been planted. The growth is uncomfortable underneath the trauma piled on top of you, and as your roots spread, you never know when you will surface or if there is one. Everything is dark right now but you have been planted. All you need to do is grow."

"How do I grow?"

"Flowers don't belong under the dirt," a soft chuckle left my lips. "So, no matter how heavy the soil gets, it will never be enough to keep them down. You are stuck under the false pretense that you have to be who you were before everything happened to you, and you don't. Everything about you has changed because of your trauma, and that is okay. You aren't worth any less than the person you used to be because of it."

Epilogue

After promising my blue-eyed boxer I would see a therapist and endless amounts of searching, I found myself in someone's office weeks later. Kinnick received a recommendation from the woman he saw during his court-ordered sessions, and after ensuring everything would be fine, I found myself giving them a call.

When the effect of my nightmares affected my attendance at work, my boss recommended taking a leave of absence. As if my anxiety couldn't get worst, I questioned if silly night terrors should push my success further away. How dare I take time away from work for not being able to grow up?

My palms rubbed over the soft cushion of the couch I sat on as I stared at the cherry oak desk in front of me, waiting for my therapist to come in. As the woman with long box braids stepped through the room, I felt comforted by the smile on her face.

Her hand extended out to me. "Hi, Boston?"

I nodded as I stood from my seated position. "Brooklyn, right?"

"Yes," she grinned. "Nice to meet you."

As she slid her bright pink mug onto the desk, I watched her fall back into the leather chair. "Thank you for coming today."

"I thought I never would," I admitted. "I thought it might be impossible."

"You walked through the door," her words soothed me. "That is enough."

Her chocolate skin glowed underneath the dim light above us. As my body relaxed into the gray material below me, I let the comfort disperse through my muscles, allowing them to relax. While the woman before me flipped through the paperwork on her desk, I contemplated how my first day would go. Just as she tossed a folder aside, I felt the confusion filling me again.

"Why are you here, Bo?"

"I need to talk to somebody about my past -"

"No," her head moved back and forth. "Why are you here? You must have a reason for scheduling an appointment. It isn't because of what happened in your past."

"I can't let go of it," I referred to my past as if she knew. "I feel like I am drowning, and I know how to swim."

"Oh, baby," she grins. "Even a professional swimmer will tell you to be careful of the riptide. You might know how to swim, but you need to get a better perspective of what waters you chose to dive into."

"Do you think my perspective of the situation is wrong?"

"No," she shrugged. "Perhaps you don't understand it clearly, though."

"I didn't say no," the tears began to sting my eyes. "When he started taking my clothes off, I didn't say no."

"When you say he, do you know who this person was?"

"At the time, he was my boyfriend."

"My friend was a different person every day," her chair squeaked as she leaned backward. "She loved flowers as much as she loved winter. Yet, the flowers she loved couldn't grow in the snow. She thought that watering the soil with hot water would make a difference. So, she did. It didn't matter if someone told her differently, she continued to do it. Sure, her flowers never grew, but she didn't care. She wasn't going to take no for an answer. Why is that, Bo?"

"Why is what?"

"Why did she continue watering the soil with hot water, even though her flowers never grew?"

A chuckle left my lips. "I don't know."

"Because it didn't matter if someone told her not to," she pointed at me. "She was going to do it anyway. So, let's get a better perspective on your situation, Bo. Had you told that boy no, would it have happened anyway?"

"I would like to think it wouldn't have."

"Oh, so did my friend," a string of laughter left her lips. "That is probably why she is outside watering her damn soil with hot water, waiting for those flowers to grow. You and I know damn well, it doesn't matter, but you will think of any way possible to make it your fault. Don't you?"

"Why would I do that?"

"Why would your boyfriend want to hurt you?"

"Because he didn't seem like the person who would do that."

"Exactly," she tapped her pen against the desk. "Something inside of you wants it to be your fault because you can't imagine him hurting you. Back to my friend, what happens if you water a plant with hot water in winter?"

"It shocks the flowers?"

"Right," she smiles. "Blaming yourself for what happened doesn't make it any better. Just like watering flowers with hot water in the cold. It doesn't change anything."

A tear rolled down my cheek. "There were other people in the room, recording what was happening. Why didn't they help me?"

I watched her eyebrows furrow. "I can't answer that for you."

"My drink was roofied, and my boyfriend raped me," I choked. "Other people watched it happen and spread the video around to my classmates."

"Bad things happen for no reason at all," she sighed. "Those bad things happen to really good people -"

"What if I am not a good person?"

"What makes you think that?"

"I've hurt everyone because of the anger I feel."

"That makes you a bad person?"

"It doesn't make me a good person."

"My friend has a child," she diverted the conversation. "He has seen multiple doctors over the years to control his anxiety. The only way he can think clearly is if he is listening to music. Not to mention, the music has to be so loud you can barely hear anybody talking. Do you know why it has to be so loud?"

"No," I shake my head.

"Because he told my friend, 'mommy, I can't hear the voices in my head when the music is loud," she frowned. "So, when my friend is driving with her kid, their music catches the attention of bystanders. They blame her for being a teenager who had a kid too young. How dare she blasts her music with a child in the car?"

"But her kid?"

"Yeah, but that's the thing, no one knows about her kid," she reminded me. "They don't know loud music silences his voices. Why doesn't my friend care when these people judge her?"

"Because they don't know about her kid?"

"Because it doesn't matter what other people assume about her," she spoke. "At night, she rests her head knowing that someone else calling her a bad mom doesn't make her one. She doesn't blame those people either because they don't understand what they do not know. So, do you believe you are a bad person or are the people around you misinformed?"

"It doesn't excuse my actions, though."

"It doesn't have to," she never skipped a beat. "As long as you realize you aren't a bad person. The trauma you carry makes you react to things differently."

"I want to get back to who I was -"

"Oh, see, you can't."

"Why?"

"Can trees pick up their fallen leaves or flowers their petals?"

"No?"

"That isn't a trick question, babe."

"No, they can't."

"Why is that?"

"They will grow new ones."

"Exactly," she grins. "They will grow new ones. You are still the same person you used to be, but you are going through things like trees go through seasons. The things around you change, but you remain the same."

"Why is it that I used to love certain things but I despise them now?"

"As in?"

"I used to love taking photos, but I used to take photos when I dated him, now I can't pick up a camera."

"What do you love to do now?"

"Write."

"It is okay to fall out of love with things," she shrugged. "It's like growing up. I played with barbies. Bo, I haven't touched one of those dolls since I was eight. Instead, I fell in love with reading. We grow out of things and that's okay."

"So, you think I am growing? You don't think it is because of him?"

"Oh, it may very well be because of him," a sigh left her lips. "Instead of you falling out of love with photography, it felt like it had been ripped away. You never got an easy transition, it just happened."

"Let me tell you about another friend," she winked, making a string of laughter fall from my lips. "She loved collecting One Direction posters. Her whole room was covered in different pictures. One day, after school, she came home to a dumpster in her yard. Her single mom explained there had been nothing she could do. Because her mom didn't pay rent, all of her stuff had been ruined. The police only granted her little time to pack the essential items, but because they had been evicted, she didn't have time for anything else."

"What happened to her posters?"

"As much as she wanted to salvage them, they had been ruined in the dumpster," she sucked in a deep breath. "She spent years collecting those posters, but when she realized it would be difficult to do it again, she stopped buying the magazines. It only reminded her of what happened. See, it wasn't that she fell out of love with it, she let what happened to her ruin the good memories."

"Do you think that is why I struggle with photography?"

"Does it bother you that you don't take photos anymore?"

"I am not sure, but it is something I realized I don't do anymore."

"Sometimes it's okay to get lost," her words sounded promising.

A chuckle left my lips. "I think I am lost."

"That's okay," a grin grew on her lips. "That is when the best adventures happen."

www.ingramcontent.com/pod-product-compliance
Lightning Source LLC
Chambersburg PA
CBHW070631170726
48291CB00003B/965